BEACH HAPPENS

Hawaii Heat Series Book Two

Jamie K. Schmidt

FREE book

Thank you for picking up this book. I hope you enjoy it.

If you'd like to keep up-to-date on my new releases and other fun things, please subscribe to my newsletter and get a FREE book

Be a VIP Reader and have a chance to win monthly prizes, free books and up-to-date information.

Click here for your free book:
https://dl.bookfunnel.com/w9gnkxp12u

To Carrie Arbuckle & Amanda Barnes, my friends since elementary school. We should have a sleepover soon and play Monopoly.

Thank you Mom and Auntie for helping proofread. Tracy & Mary, I really appreciate your spot on edits and for not rolling your eyes at my tight deadlines.

And as always, a huge shout out to my MTBs for all the support!

Table of Contents

Chapter One...5

Chapter Two..11

Chapter Three..26

Chapter Four...39

Chapter Five...51

Chapter Six..65

Chapter Seven 82

Chapter Eight..92

Chapter Nine 98

Chapter Ten...105

Chapter Eleven...115

Chapter Twelve 127

Chapter Thirteen...137

Chapter Fourteen 145

Chapter Fifteen..157

Chapter Sixteen 172

Chapter Seventeen...181

Chapter Eighteen 192

Chapter Nineteen...198

Chapter Twenty 203

Chapter Twenty-One 210

Epilogue 218

Chapter One

MICHAELA HARRIS PEEKED OUT INTO the church. It was full of people, half of whom she didn't recognize. Business associates of her parents, most likely. She tugged up the bodice of her wedding gown.

*Don't cry. Do **not** cry.*

"He probably had a last minute, urgent phone call," Corrine said, in a tone that was supposed to be soothing.

Michaela's other three bridesmaids, Gerald's cousins, were smoking outside and arguing over which of the groomsmen they were going to bang at the reception.

"Your brother is never late," Michaela said, not turning from the door. The people were already whispering among themselves and craning their necks to catch a glimpse of any of the wedding party.

In fact, Gerald was almost pathological about being on time. He once gave her the cold shoulder all night because they arrived at a corporate function five minutes late. They had gotten stuck in traffic, but since Michaela had been driving, it was all her fault.

"He'll be here." Corrine patted her shoulder and then scurried out of the vestibule with her phone already in her hand.

Michaela wished her wedding gown had pockets. She could catch up on some emails to distract her from this fiasco. She glanced around, but she didn't see her purse. Her mother probably had it. There was no way in hell she was going to try and find her mother right now. She was probably having martinis from a flask with a few of her friends by the baptismal pool.

Not that kind of a pool party, Mom.

"Where is he?" Her father burst in, looking like a pissed off waiter in his custom fitted tuxedo.

Michaela closed the door so the entire church couldn't hear him. "I don't know."

She hadn't seen Gerald since he kissed her goodbye last night. He told her he was going to go back to his place and have an early night.

"Carl said he wasn't at his condo when he went to pick him up this morning."

The best man had been frantic, and showed up at her apartment looking for him. It was her first clue that this day was going to go right into the shitter.

Gerald's phone went to voice mail and he hadn't called any of them back all morning.

"Did the two of you have a fight?" her father growled, looming over her.

"No." Michaela forced herself to meet his eyes and not step back as he invaded her personal space—which wasn't easy considering she was wearing a crinoline and her dress resembled a bell.

She had told herself this morning that Gerald must have lost his phone, or it was out of battery and he was already at the church. But he hadn't been here when they arrived.

Her father sighed explosively and stomped around, opening up doors and glaring through them as if he expected Gerald to be playing hide and seek.

"We checked the hospitals." Michaela trailed off into a whisper when she realized she wouldn't be able to keep the tears out of her voice.

Her father stormed out of the room.

Thanks for the kind words and support.

But that was her father. More concerned about his own image than his daughter being abandoned at the altar.

How was she going to face everyone on Monday? The jilted bride. She could see the smirks on the faces of her co-workers and hear their "compassionate" platitudes.

He was a little out of your reach, anyway.

If he's anything like his father, he'll be bald by forty.

You're better off without him. He likes younger women anyway.

He did too. His last girlfriend was a freshman in college. She dumped him for a bass player in a grunge band. Michaela's father set them up shortly after.

If Gerald was so unhappy, why didn't he say something last night? Hell, why did he even ask her to marry him if he didn't want to go through with it?

They were good together. The sex was predictable, but they were compatible. They were both attorneys, so they understood the long hours and the pressure. They both wanted to make partner in their individual firms. They were a good fit. It made sense that they get married. Both their families had been ecstatic when they announced their engagement. It had been fun to bask in the glow of her father's approval for once.

Michaela looked at the clock on the wall. He was two hours late. Gerald was either dead or not coming.

Corrine came back in and handed Michaela her cell phone. "I think you need to see this."

Looking down at the phone, she saw a text conversation between Gerald and his sister.

I CAN'T DO THIS. Gerald had typed.\

So much for the being dead theory.

YOU CAN. YOU JUST HAVE COLD FEET. Corrine had texted back.

I DON'T LOVE HER.

Michaela's knees buckled and she sagged against the wall for support. She took in a shaky breath. It shouldn't have been a surprise. They never said those words to each other. They weren't emotional people. They were analytical. They liked numbers. Love was what you watched on television and in the movies. But it still hurt to see it there in the harsh glow of the cell phone screen.

Gerald should have told her this last night. He could have saved her this humiliation. He might not love her, but he should have been her friend. He should have been here, and then they could tell their guests together.

She passed the phone back to Corrine, not bothering to read the rest of the conversation.

"I told him it didn't matter," Corrine said. "That he was being selfish."

Michaela flinched. *It did matter.*

"I told him that he needed to be here."

"What did he say?"

Corrine sighed. "He's not coming."

"No." Her father's face was red and mottled, having just come back into the room to hear the last part.

"Dad, settle down. You're going to have a stroke." Michaela held his arm so he stayed in one place. She flipped up her veil. "I think we need to tell everyone to just head to the reception."

He shook her off. "Gerald Stone will be here. The merger won't go on without him."

For a moment, she was amused that her father was calling her marriage a merger. It was an accurate description. Then she realized he was talking about the actual corporate merger between Harris Industries and Stone Mechanics.

"Wait," Michaela said. "What do you mean?"

"I mean if the Stones want my company, they have to take my daughter too."

Michaela reeled back in shock. "I'm not a pawn in your corporate deals. This is the twenty-first century. I am an attorney, not chattel."

"This has nothing to do with you."

Michaela blinked at him. "My marriage has nothing to do with me?"

"Keep your voice down," he ordered.

She flung open the door and swished out down the aisle as fast as her behemoth gown could carry her. The organ player started playing a hopeful few bars of the Wedding March.

"Can it," Michaela snarled at him and the music stopped with a heavy pound on the keyboard.

"Michaela stop." Her father stomped on her train, but since it was eight feet long it took a while to stop her from going forward.

She glared at him over her shoulder. "Ladies and Gentlemen," Michaela said to the people sitting in the pews on either side of her. "I'm sorry to inform you that Gerald Stone has decided to breach his verbal contract with my father. There will not be a wedding today. However, the Malibu Beach House has a wonderful cocktail hour starting—" She looked at her wrist where

9

she wasn't wearing a watch. "—about now. So please enjoy a wonderful dinner and a Venetian table that will make you weep, courtesy of Harris Industries."

Michaela whirled back and stepped on her own train. "Out of my way, old man," she said to her father, pushing him back a few steps when he didn't move.

He only gaped at her in shock.

"Get me out of this thing," she snarled to Corrine and her bridesmaids, invoking Bridezilla for the first time in her long engagement.

Her mother came sloshing in just as Michaela was stepping out of the yards and yards of fabric.

"Oh honey, what are you going to do?"

"I'm going to Maui," Michaela said, padding over in her high priced underwear to her mother. Taking her purse from under her mother's arms, she shuffled until she found her honeymoon tickets.

Ripping up Gerald's boarding pass, Michaela tossed that and her bouquet into the trash can. It might have been overkill when she dumped one of the lit candles on top.

And had she been thinking clearly at the time, she wouldn't have stomped out to her car in her corset and heels. Especially, since everyone and their brother had a cell phone camera out.

But Michaela didn't care. She slammed her car door and screeched out of the church's parking lot.

"Palekaiko Beach Resort, here I come."

Chapter Two

MICHAELA DRANK ON THE PLANE. She drank too much. After six hours of screwdrivers, she pretty much had heartburn and a throbbing headache, but not heartache. She was over the horror of her failed wedding and the security at LAX.

She had been selected for a random screening because—of course she did. They found traces on her hands of something that scanned as bomb making material. WTF? Really? Michaela had been escorted into the private room for a pat down.

It had been really hard keeping all the sarcastic things she wanted to say in check. But after a humiliating and intrusive pat down, Michaela was deemed non-threatening and allowed to catch her plane. Turns out the hand cream she used triggered the false positive. Next time, she'd live with the chapped hands.

When the plane touched down in Kahului, Michaela couldn't wait to pour herself into a taxi and go to the resort. So she stumbled to baggage claim, rolling her carry-on behind her and waited for her luggage to come out.

And waited.

And waited.

Until all the luggage had been claimed.

"No," she said, by this time horribly sober and exhausted to the point of tears.

Yes.

The airline had lost her bags. After another hour of waiting and waiting some more, Michaela was told to go to her hotel, and when her bag showed up they would put it in a taxi and send it to her.

Unfortunately, they were a little vague on when that would be.

Michaela got the name of the supervisor to talk to if her bags didn't show up by morning.

When she finally got to the Palekaiko Resort, Michaela leapt out of the cab and considered kissing the ground. But with all the chickens she saw, she was afraid of the chicken poop. Chickens seemed to have the right of way and no one looked twice at them.

Staggering to the lobby, she debated sinking into a chair and crying. But she decided that could wait until she got into the privacy of her own room.

"*Aloha*," the desk clerk said. He was a slim, handsome Hawaiian man. His name tag said Hani.

"*Aloha*," Michaela said with feeling. "Checking in. Reservation should be under Stone." Her married name, had there been a wedding.

Glancing outside, she could just barely see the ocean. Damn, she should have brought her surfboard. But then again, the airline would have lost that too. Gerald hadn't wanted her to bring it.

"What am I supposed to do while you're surfing?" he had whined. "It's our honeymoon."

Putting her elbow on the desk, she rested her chin on her hand. Hani frowned and typed furiously. All of a sudden, she was bathed in a cold sweat.

"What's wrong?" Michaela asked. But like with the secret AHA! moment in the movie *Sixth Sense*, she pieced it together a moment before the big reveal.

That son-of-a-bitch!

"Um," Hani said, scratching his head. "It looks like that reservation was cancelled yesterday. We had to a charge fifty percent because of the late notice, but the guy didn't care."

"What guy?" she said between her teeth.

"Mr. Stone. Gerald Stone."

"Oh no," she said.

"Ma'am?" he asked.

Michaela took a deep, shuddering breath. "I was supposed to have gotten married yesterday." She blinked rapidly. No crying. She was a hard ass attorney. "He decided to call the wedding off."

Damn it. Gerald didn't get to have this type of power over me.

She was in paradise. She may not have her luggage, a husband or a honeymoon, but she had a credit card and she was not afraid to use it. This was her first vacation in five years and she would enjoy herself. Even if she had to max her Visa out to do it.

Swallowing her anger, Michaela needed a minute and looked above Hani's head until she calmed down. Hani didn't deserve her bitchiness. There was a framed picture on the wall of a smiling Hawaiian woman giving the shaka two-handed.

Hang loose.

Chill.

For some reason Pololena Kamaka, employee-of-the-month, and her happy face gave her the strength to look back at Hani.

"I guess he decided to cancel the honeymoon too and didn't tell me." She hoped the smile she flashed him was more "devil may care" than a grimace.

Hani looked horrified.

Michaela felt a little sorry for the kid. Straightening her shoulders and mentally pulling on her big girl panties, she said, "Do you have any open rooms available? I'll be happy to rebook."

Biting his lip, Hani started typing again. "I'll check. But I know we're full, and we were able to give away your room on a last minute deal to a local." He looked up and winced. "Uh, we have all you can eat and drink specials. We're pretty popular."

Michaela nodded.

After a few minutes of searching and Hani muttering things in Hawaiian, her spirits sank. She looked at her phone and wasn't surprised at all to find out she was out of battery. Served her right for playing Candy Crush on the plane.

"Do you have a place I can recharge this?" she asked.

"Sure," he said. "Give it to me and I can plug it in back here."

Michaela handed him her phone.

"I'm sorry. We don't have anything. A whole block of rooms are being renovated, and they're not ready for guests."

"I understand." Michaela sighed. It figured, with the way her luck was going. "Do you know of any other places that might have an opening last minute?"

He winced. "It's the state surfing championship this week. Pretty much everything is going to be booked."

Don't panic.

Hani must have saw it on her face anyway. "But let me call around for you. Other hotels might have cancellations they're looking to fill."

"I'd really appreciate it."

"In the meantime, please help yourself to the buffet." He reached under the desk and handed her a free coupon.

Michaela hadn't realized how hungry she was. She almost swayed. "You're an awesome man."

"As soon as I find a hotel for you, I'll send someone to find you with the information. Do you have a price limit?"

"If we can keep it around the same price as my old reservation that would be great, but I understand beggars can't be choosers."

"Roger dat," he said. He gave her a map and showed her the path to get to the buffet. "I'll keep your cell phone safe. No worries. I can hold your luggage here too." He craned his neck.

"Yeah, well you could if the airline had remembered to put it on the plane. It's dancing around LAX somewhere."

Hani reached back under the desk and handed her another coupon.

Good for two free Piña Coladas.

"You married?" she asked him. "I've got the dress."

He laughed nervously. "I got a boyfriend."

She winked at him. "He's a lucky man." Michaela handed him her carry-on. At least there was a change of clothes, her bathing suit and whatever makeup she could fit in a quart size baggie in there. None of which she needed at the moment and she was sick of schlepping the stupid thing around. Then she paused. Her engagement ring was in there too, a Vera Wang design Gerald got a Jared's. She had loved it. It had hurt to take it off her finger, because she had worn it every day for two years. She should really dig it out and put it on, just so no one stole it.

Fuck it. Fuck him.

As far as she was concerned, that ring was cursed. If someone wanted all that bad karma stored in it, they were welcome.

15

Michaela strolled through the courtyard. The sun was setting with a dramatic palette of pinks and oranges. People gathered on the beach to watch, holding hands and laughing. She wasn't in that place in her head yet where she could enjoy a beautiful sunset. She was more in a headspace of toss herself in the ocean and let the waves batter her around for a bit. But she knew better than to do that in strange waters. Sharks came out this time of night anyway.

She shuddered. She had seen a few shark attacks in Malibu and had even been in the water when the life guards called everyone in. She was terrified of them, but it wouldn't keep her out of the water. Shark attacks weren't all that common. They were just memorable. Michaela had surfed up and down the California coast for most of her life, and had only seen sharks a handful of times.

Damn Gerald anyway. As soon as she got settled in a hotel, she was going to find out where to rent a surf board.

The buffet was pretty much empty, except for a man who sat at a table with a lap top. He was scowling into it and had his phone up to his ear. He looked up when she passed by him, did a double take, and then something on the phone caught his attention.

"No. Damn it. I don't care if it is two in the morning. The fucking servers are down and you need to find out why before we open for business in a few hours. I can't open my fucking files."

She grimaced. Sounds like she wasn't the only one who the bluebird of happiness shit on. Still, she'd trade his bad day for hers. Of course that would mean she'd be with Gerald right now as his wife, and her case load would be in a black hole somewhere.

Nah, I'm good after all.

The relief hit her like a two by four in the knees. She'd dodged a bullet. Her marriage to Gerald wouldn't have been anything but business. And Michaela wanted more than that. Shit, she *deserved* more than that.

16

Still, the burn of humiliation hadn't quite left yet. Blinking back tears, she took a seat where she could see a little bit of the beach, when it wasn't blocked by palm trees. After handing in her coupon to the waitress, she went up to the buffet table.

The man was drumming his fingers on the table, a tic that reminded her of Gerald and she controlled a shudder. They had been friends, or at least she thought so. It hurt that he felt he couldn't have been honest with her.

The buffet was overwhelming with all of the choices, some of which Michaela had never heard of like haupia pudding and lomi lomi salmon. Her stomach growled. She had been on the diet from hell for the last six months to make sure her wedding dress would fit perfectly. Another thing to resent Gerald for. She gave up chocolate for that man!

Dick!

She made a mental note to try everything at some point, but started off with a large fruit salad and some Hawaiian rolls stuffed with Spam.

Bread!

She got two coffees because she figured once she sat down, she wasn't going to get up again until they kicked her out. Michaela couldn't decide between the chocolate espresso cake smothered in whipped cream and the triple chocolate brownie doused with thick caramel sauce. So she got both.

Fuck it! I'm on vacation.

"I'm not paying you to give me excuses. Fix the damn thing and then figure out how it happened so I never have to end my day again, wondering if I lost all my work," the man barked.

Michaela rolled her eyes. He sounded like a real prince to work for. Then again, it wasn't her files that were currently swimming around in cyberspace.

While he was distracted, she got a good eyeful of him. His face was just short of pretty, a broken nose marring what could have been a model's profile. He had a wide, sensual mouth and long, elegant fingers. He made her a little giddy, but that could just be hysteria creeping in disguised as exhaustion.

"Two hours." He tossed his phone on the table in disgust and rubbed his palm over his face.

Michaela looked at the phone a little longingly. She wished her phone was charged. She'd like to give Gerald hell. The last time she checked her phone, he still hadn't texted or called.

The man started typing, his strong jaw set. She didn't envy who was going to get the email he was sending. Maybe she should send Gerald an email? That way she could get everything out without being interrupted. Eating the desserts first, she licked her spoon clean with vindictive glee. Take that, Spanx.

Dear Dickhead,

Fuck you, you piece of shit.

Michaela shook her head. Never put anything in writing that you don't want read in a court of law. She should probably wait until she wasn't emotionally overwrought from a horrendous few days.

She pushed away the feelings of loneliness because if she didn't, she would start to cry. If they couldn't find her a hotel room, maybe she could rent a minivan and see if she could pay someone to let her park in their driveway.

How was your honeymoon, Michaela?

Great. I spent it alone and homeless.

Stuffing her mouth with the sweet and savory bread, she forced herself to chew away the bad thoughts, but they kept creeping up. This vacation was supposed to have been more than just a honeymoon. It was the first time off she'd taken in five years. It was supposed to be full of booze-fueled sex and laughter. Now, she'd be lucky if she was going to have a place to shower.

Don't panic.

Concentrating on taking deep breaths, she speared a pineapple and her mouth exploded with pleasure. Oh yum. That taste might just have redeemed the day. Perfectly sweet and not sour, it was the best pineapple she'd ever tasted.

The bad feelings subsided enough that she was able to see perspective. She wasn't at work. She wasn't married to a man who didn't love her. And she was going to surf all day tomorrow. A soft breeze from the ocean, ruffled her hair as if to say, *Aloha.*

Finishing the last of the bread, Michaela pushed the tray away and the bus boy immediately came and took it away from her. If she had her laptop, she could answer a few emails so she wasn't so slammed when she got back, but she had deliberately left it at home. If she couldn't bring her surfboard, then Gerald couldn't bring his computer. Of course, that meant she couldn't either so it was sitting on her desk back in California. He had argued with her about it. He had clients in Hawaii. If he could meet with them, he could write off his honeymoon as a tax deduction.

That should have been her first clue that it would all end in tears.

Taking a sip of her coffee, Michaela watched the angry businessman again. He was really good looking. Flicking her gaze to his hands, she didn't see a ring on his finger. Not that it mattered. Why would she care? She'd had enough of snide workaholics. He was in Hawaii for Pete's sake. He should be out on the beach with the rest of them. Or hanging out in the Tiki bar with an equally gorgeous woman on his arm.

Michaela was determined to put the mainland behind her for two weeks. She wasn't an overworked attorney struggling for partner. No, here she was just going to be a surfer girl. Her priorities were going to be rad waves and parties. She didn't have to be alone, if she didn't want to be.

The man ran his fingers through his blond hair in frustration. It made it stick up in an adorable mess. She felt a little tickle along her spine when he looked up and caught her staring at him. His eyes were a warm shade of green, full of intelligence and ire.

"Get everything sorted out?" she asked, deciding to brazen through it, even though she felt her cheeks warm in embarrassment.

He blew out a sigh. "It's hard being in the wrong time zone." He closed his laptop with a snap. "I'm Marcus."

"Michaela," she said.

"I'd offer you something to drink, but I see you're two fisting it already." He motioned to the two cups of coffee.

"I can share," she pushed one across the table. She could use a little bit of company, and he was really easy on the eyes.

"I can get my own." He smiled and went over to the machine.

Michaela did a double take. He had a fine ass and his shoulders were nice and broad. Should she really be talking to strange men? No. But she was sick of her own company.

Marcus came back with two mugs of his own. "Mind if I join you?"

"Not at all." She noticed he had some pretty impressive biceps too.

"Did you just get here?"

Michaela nodded. "Yeah, I'm beat." Which was probably why she was ogling him like he was a Playgirl centerfold.

"You'll like it here," he said. "The staff takes good care of you."

"I'm not staying here," she said, feeling a little sad that she wasn't. She had picked out this resort because of the location to Black Rock and the Whaler's Village shopping mall. It seemed to have everything Gerald and she liked. But apparently Michaela didn't have a clue what that prick wanted. He had suggested a luxurious resort down in Wailea, but she had a sneaking suspicion that's where his clients were, so she convinced him that staying on the Kaanapali strip was a much better choice. She wondered if the Kaimana Beach Resort that Gerald wanted to stay at would have been able to find her an opening or if they would have called her a cab back to the airport.

"Where are you staying?"

Michaela raised an eyebrow. Hot or not, he didn't get to have that information. Of course, she had no idea either, but that was beside the point.

"Why do you want to know?"

He smiled apologetically. "Sorry, didn't mean to be nosy. I live here part of the year, so I was going to recommend a few things to do."

"It's okay," she said. "What do you do for fun?"

"Spreadsheets," he deadpanned, surprising a laugh out of her.

"Exciting."

"Yeah, that's me. Mr. Excitement. How about you?"

That was the thing, Michaela wasn't sure. It had been such a long time since she had fun she had almost forgotten how. "I've got to say a good pivot table makes my toes tingle," she quipped instead. It was even a little true.

His answering grin was like a shot of tequila.

"What do you do for a living?" he asked.

Ugh, really? Why was it always work, work, work?

Michaela didn't want to talk business. She knew his type. If she told him she was a lawyer, he'd react one of two ways. He'd either start drilling her with questions, looking for free legal advice or he'd act condescending.

"I'm a surfer," she blurted out. She looked down into her coffee cup. Maybe they added crazy pills to it.

"Well, you've come to the right place." Marcus waved his coffee cup. "Hawaii, I mean. Not necessarily this resort. Best waves in the world."

"I hope so. I can't wait to hit the water tomorrow."

He nodded. "You got a great choice of beaches."

She had beaches at home too. But it was nice to get away from

it all. Maybe by the time she got home, everything would have blown over. At the very least, Michaela hoped her father's merger went through with Gerald's family while she was gone. She'd like to never speak to her ex again. She tamped down her anger. No sense getting all riled up again.

"Why did you choose Maui, though instead of the Big Island?"

Yeah, Michaela. Why?

She cleared her throat. "Too overcrowded. Too fast paced. I'm sick of the rat race, you know?"

As she said it, she was surprised that it was actually true.

He blinked at her and nodded. "Yeah, yeah I think I do." But then his phone rang and he looked down at it. "I'm sorry. I've got to get this."

Her lips twisted into a smile. "Good luck with the servers."

"Have a nice vacation, Michaela. *Aloha*." He winked at her and walked back to his laptop. It didn't look like he got good news because he packed up and left shortly after. He didn't even glance back at her.

"And so he walked out of my life," Michaela said, more dejected by the stranger leaving than Gerald.

She had just finished her second cup of coffee when a woman approached her. "Ms. Stone?"

"Not in this lifetime. I'm Michaela Harris." Michaela said. "Did Hani send you?"

"Yes. I'm Amelia Kincaide. I'm the manager of the resort. May I sit?"

"Sure." Michaela was a little jittery from the coffee or maybe it was nerves.

"I've got some bad news."

"Hit me with it." At this point, Michaela was numb. Besides, she still had coupons for two free pina coladas and her credit cards. She'd find a way to enjoy Hawaii.

"I can't find a hotel room, a condo, a timeshare or someone's couch for you to stay on." Amelia's eyes crossed in frustration. "I even tried the Y, but Camp Keanae's booked, unless you have a tent stashed in the overnight bag."

"Damn, you don't beat around the bush." She reminded Michaela of Zooey Deschanel in that TV show the *New Girl*.

"I think your ex fiancé is a dill hole."

Michaela cracked a grin. "I've been thinking more flaming asshole, but we can agree to disagree."

Amelia bit her nail. "I don't have any rooms available that are up to snuff for a paying customer. But I do have rooms that are under renovation. This is a unique situation for us and normally I wouldn't even consider offering a room that isn't up to our quality standards, but…"

Michaela held up a hand. "Does it have a bed and a shower?"

"Yes, but no air conditioning and the room needs to be painted and the floor doesn't have a carpet or tile."

"I'll take it."

Amelia sagged in relief. "I was hoping you would say that."

"Why?"

"Because your shit heel ex shouldn't get to ruin your vacation. He's done enough damage."

Tears threatened to overwhelm Michaela at the vehemence in Amelia's voice. This was the first time anyone had gotten angry on her behalf. Sure, her father had been pissed, but it was all about him. Her mother was worried about the gossip. Gerald's family couldn't even look her in the eye. Not to mention that rat bastard himself still hadn't called her to explain. Of course, her phone had been dead for the past hour, so maybe he had.

"I can't thank you enough," Michaela said.

"Don't worry. Once the surfing tournaments are over this week, we'll have some rooms available. There's no charge for the renovation room, and I'm upgrading you to a suite as soon as I can."

"So I'm staying?" she grinned.

"Welcome to Palekaiko Beach Resort," Amelia said. "*Aloha.*"

"Thank you. Or should I say *mahalo*?"

Chapter Three

MARCUS KINCAIDE STOOD ON HIS BALCONY and looked out over the long stretch of Maui's Kaanapali Beach. He really needed to get back to New York, but days like this it was hard to remember why.

Marcus snorted. If he wasn't careful, he was going to wind up in a hammock next to his brother. They could be Dude and...Marcus shrugged. He'd have to come up with another stoner surfer name. He wasn't growing a beard, though. That shit itched.

When his cell phone rang, he thought about ignoring it. But in the end, it was reflex to look down to see who was calling. It was his arch enemy, Tetsuo. Maybe thinking about him as a super villain was over-the-top, but he had made their lives hell this past year after kidnapping Amelia, his brother's girlfriend and now wife, and railroading their efforts to renovate the Palekaiko Resort.

His sister-in-law could deal with Tetsuo. She was always complaining about wanting more responsibility. If Amelia didn't have Tetsuo eating out of the palm of her head by midday, he'd put on a clam shell bra and grass skirt.

Marcus shut off his phone. At least Baxter got the servers up and running under the deadline. Marcus had backed up his data and found he didn't want to spend another minute working.

Michaela, the gorgeous brunette who had been giving him bedroom eyes last night, inspired him. He was going surfing. She had haunted his thoughts all night. If he hadn't been so twisted up about losing his data, she might have woken up in bed next to him this morning.

He was hoping to remedy that as soon as possible. There was something going on with her that he couldn't put a finger on, but he wished he had stayed to talk with her last night. She hadn't been a party girl, or a surfer chick, or even a beach bunny. She was different. After five minutes of talking with her, he hadn't wished for a strong drink or looked for an escape before his brains leaked out of his ears.

Marcus had been enjoying their conversation, when he wasn't wondering what her mouth tasted like and if she would like kisses that lasted hours. It figured that business had reared its ugly head and interrupted what might have been the beginning of a very interesting affair.

Marcus grabbed his long board. The small waves were mushy lately and he wasn't good enough with the short board to keep up with the locals. As it was, it had taken him over a year to get them to warm up to him in the lineup. And even then, if one *haole* dropped in on them, or worse paddled around them, it was Marcus who had to hear about it.

Attaching the board to the top of his car, Marcus drove down to Honolua Bay. It was windy and that might not bode well for the waves, but he didn't care. In New York right now, it was eighteen degrees and sleeting. Last week, a nor'easter dropped a foot and a half of snow on the city.

In Maui, on the other hand, it was eighty degrees and sunny. Anything that he needed to do, he could do from a wireless café once the sun got too hot or the waves went flat. Why did he have to go back to New York again?

Marcus didn't have an answer, which was why he hadn't been back except for quick visits in two years.

"Keanu," he tried out, pulling the rearview mirror down to see if he could pull off looking like a Keanu. He couldn't. Too uptight.

"Takukmi," he growled. No, he was too blond for that one.

"Bodhi." Maybe.

"Brody." Better.

That was it. He gave himself the shaka sign in the mirror and then fixed it back to the correct place. He could be Brody, the surfer dude. Then, maybe he could find Michaela and he could convince her that he wanted out of the rat race too. But first he had to convince himself.

He'd have to practice with Samuel talking slang and pidgin to fit in, but as a first step he could throw out his corporate suits and concentrate living the good life. Except at the next stop light, he turned his phone back on and checked his messages. Not bad. He lasted a full half hour with it off. Baby steps.

Parking on the street, he locked his wallet and his phone in the trunk and left his doors unlocked so no one had to smash his windows to see that there wasn't anything to steal.

Calling Honolua Bay a beach was a stretch. There wasn't any powdery sand like Kaanapali had. It was mostly rocks, but that was all right by him. Jumping in with what looked to be about a hundred other people, he paddled out past the murky water and into the clear blue ocean.

It was one of those perfect days, when the wind was blowing off shore and the waves were lining up just right. Which was a relief, because under those curls were unforgiving reef and rocks ready to cut up a surfer who wasn't paying attention. Or one who was grandstanding without the experience to back it up.

While he sat up on his board in the shoulder waiting his turn in the line, Marcus's attention was caught by a hot, female surfer. He wondered if it was Michaela or if that was wishful thinking. She had the right curves and the long black hair. Flipping into an aerial that took her above the wave, she almost did a 360, but another wave knocked her off the board.

"*Akaw!*" a voice he recognized said from off to his left.

"Hani, aren't you working today?" Marcus asked his bellmen.

"I am working. I'm just on a break," Hani said defensively.

It was nine in the morning and the resort was over a half hour away. Marcus opened his mouth to call him out on it, but decided against it. Just because he could be a dick, didn't mean he had to be one. Samuel complained he was too much of a hard ass. Well, one of them had to be. Still, he didn't want to be the boss right now—even if a part of him felt he left a limb locked in his trunk instead of his cell phone.

Hani whistled at the woman and gave her two thumbs up as she recovered her board. She paddled in their direction. It *was* Michaela. *Hot damn.* A smile stretched across his face. His day was looking up.

"Who's that?" Marcus asked, wondering if Hani knew her.

"Some *wahine* who tagged along. She's got mad skills, *ae*?"

He nodded, not wanting to take his eyes off her. She was stunning. Sleek black hair hung down her back in a ponytail and her wetsuit accentuated her full curves. She'd made his mouth water last night, but he had been too pissed off to fully concentrate on her company.

He never knew how to talk to surfer girls. He probably came across as a big square. It was like they knew he was a suit even when he wore board shorts.

"Why are you taking your break here instead of Kaanapali?" he asked, even though he was pretty sure he knew why. Same reason Marcus came all the way out here to surf. Of course, he wasn't on the clock like Hani was.

Let it go, his inner surfer, Brody, whispered.

Marcus blew out a breath.

Take the stick out your ass, brah.

He frowned, that was his brother's voice in his head. The waves at Kaanapali were gentle and mushy all the time. Out here, especially this time of year, you got a nice surf break when the water hit the reefs, if the wind was right. Still, it was a long way to go on a coffee break.

"Amelia is testing this place out as a surf excursion. So I volunteered to critique Honolua."

"Is Amelia high?" Marcus tried to get a hold of his blood pressure which just threatened to boil out his ears. "We don't have the liability insurance to bring inexperienced surfers out here."

She could have just asked me.

Hani shrugged. "So we don't bring the kooks out here. Keep the gremmies at the resort and take the duders and dudettes."

Marcus frowned. The word dude made him think of his brother, who liked to pretend he was a beach bum named Dude instead of a brilliant stock broker. His brother was a shitty surfer, though. He didn't have the patience or the temperament to wait for the wave.

"Outside!" a call came out across the water.

Marcus and Hani paddled further out of the line to avoid getting caught out by it. Looking over his shoulder to see if the Michaela was following, he nearly tipped off the board.

"Steady there, Barney," Hani said, grabbing him.

Marcus glared at the insult.

"You're going to make the Palekaiko crew look bad."

"Who else..." Marcus started to say, but then caught sight of Makoa, another of the bellmen, leaning back on the gigantic wave they had been warned about. Kai, the concierge, surfed backside on the following roller. Joely, one of the resort's maids, duck dived under another wave as she paddled in position to drop in on the next.

"Is anyone at the resort?" Marcus asked. "Aside from Amelia?" Amelia never went anywhere, unless it was out to Samuel's yacht. She was a workaholic, just like Marcus was. Only she knew how to loosen up and Marcus didn't.

His brother, on the other hand, was a beach bum, but occasionally he could step up. Marcus hoped he was helping her out today. Now, he felt bad about not taking Tetsuo's call. Maybe he should go in. But before he could decide, Michaela had paddled up next to them and for a moment, he forgot to breathe.

Damn.

She was even better looking wearing a wet suit with the salt water drying on her thick lashes.

Hani chose not to answer his questions and instead greeted the pretty brunette with a shaka. "Michaela that was badass."

"I've done better," she admitted. When she looked Marcus in the eye, he felt a punch of something stronger than lust. She had deep brown eyes that he wanted to spend hours staring into. He blamed the weird feeling in his stomach on the large wave that they rode over.

Marcus was dimly aware he was smiling like an idiot. He hoped she remembered him. "Hi, I'm…" for a ridiculous moment, he almost said Brody. But then Hani cut him off.

"This is one of the *kahunas* that own the resort I work for."

"Dude?" She had a pretty smile to go with those curves. He wasn't the only one on the water to notice either.

Marcus scowled. Crap. He hadn't even made an impression. "No, we met last night. At the buffet?"

31

"I know," she said. "I just heard that the owner's name was Dude."

"Co-owner. I'm his brother. I'm just Marcus." Not Brody. Not a beach bum. Just a misplaced New Yorker trying to fit in a world that was so alien to him, it could be on Mars. "That was pretty impressive out there." He shook her hand like she was a business contact.

Her eyes twinkled at him and he was enchanted at the laugh lines at the corners of them. Marcus wanted to see her laugh. But all he could come up with was, "So where did you learn to surf?"

"California, but I've been all over."

"Ever surfed the Mavericks?"

"Shit no," she swore.

It charmed the hell out of him.

Michaela shook her head. "People have drowned out there. I just can't see risking death over a wave."

"Aw c'mon," Hani said. "You gotta live life to the fullest. Maybe Marcus over here can pull a few strings and get you invited to surf Jaws?"

"No." Michaela shuddered. "Any wave you have to tow me out to on a jet ski, I don't want to catch."

"*Kahuna*, over here has done it," Hani said, elbowing him.

Don't help me. Marcus grimaced.

"Yeah?" She lit up a bit and he had to hand it to Hani, he had her attention at least. "What's it like?"

That was better than Amelia's, "Are you out of your *freaking* mind?"

"Intense." He grinned sheepishly. "My brother and I took a boat out and we had a team of jet skis. I had on a wetsuit with an inflatable air bladder in case I got pounded under on a wipeout. The waves were amazing that day, so I was feeling pretty confident."

Marcus noticed that her eyes got wide and she leaned forward. He wished they were alone instead of in the middle of the ocean with a bunch of surfers jeering at each other.

"How big were the waves?"

"About twenty-five feet. We pinged the buoys the night before. I'm not suicidal. That's my limit."

"That's still pretty impressive," Michaela said. "Ten is pretty scary in my opinion."

Hani snorted. "I did a fifty-footer once in Kauai. You should have seen them."

Michaela shook her head. "I can't even imagine something that big."

"It makes you realize that the ocean just tolerates you." Marcus didn't even want to be on the boat when those enormous rollers came crashing in.

Hani shook his head. "My cousin does big wave surfing all the time. He ain't right in the head."

"Before or after the wave pounded him?"

"Who can tell?" Hani shrugged.

"Speaking of Jaws," Marcus said, "Did you hear about the fifteen foot tiger shark the other day in Ma'alaea?"

Hani grimaced. "Took a big bite out of the SUP."

"SUP?" Michaela asked.

"Stand up paddleboard," Marcus filled in. "It was about twelve feet long from what I heard."

"Tiger shark," Hani said.

"How deep was the water?" Michaela asked.

Marcus smiled. "Where it happened it was about twenty feet, but it was only forty yards from the shore."

Michaela's mouth opened and shut. "That's too close for comfort," she finally said and tucked her feet up on her board. "Do they ever come around here?"

"Sure," Marcus said, ignoring Hani's frown. "We had a six footer a few weeks ago. If you get cut up on the reef, get out of the water as soon as you can."

She swallowed hard and he felt a little bad. Marcus realized the conversation was making her nervous. Nothing like talking about an apex predator when your feet are dangling in its waters. He had been trying to show off his knowledge of the place with a fascination for the danger. It looked like he wound up scaring the crap out of her instead. Way to go, Marcus. Bet Brody wouldn't have done that.

Marcus sighed.

Hani was next to catch the wave. As soon as he stood up, another wave crashed over him and he went down.

"Tough break," Michaela said.

He nodded. Sometimes it was like that. Wait for an hour. Up for a second and get pounded.

"So what happened?" Michaela said. "At Jaws."

Marcus wanted to impress her. He really did. But he couldn't lie for shit. "I was up for about ten seconds. Hit the middle and got locked in. The wave collapsed and I got absolutely crushed. It was epic. Then came a cleanup set of waves that broke in front of the line. The entire line got cleared." Marcus demonstrated with his hands the wave crashing down and sending the surfers ass over teakettle.

Clapping her hands over her cheeks, she cried, "Oh no."

"It was like being inside of a washer during the spin cycle. But what a rush. Even getting towed back to the boat on the sled was a trip." He grinned at her, and her eyes shone with longing. Marcus wondered if he could make her look like that over wine and dinner.

"I wouldn't have the nerve, but I'd like to see it."

"How long are you here for?" he asked.

"A couple of weeks."

"Do you want to head out to Pe'ahi sometime?" Marcus asked. "We can take the boat or drive down if you want. I know some people. We can just watch if you don't want to surf." He hoped she said boat so he could show off his yacht. What's the point of having a big boat, if you couldn't use it to seduce pretty girls?

"Maybe," she said, looking down at her board. She was blushing. "I'm not sure what my plans are. I'm kind of playing everything by ear. My life's been a little crazy lately."

Marcus tried to play it cool. He should get her number, but neither of them had cell phones on. They rolled on the waves, getting closer to position. "It's nice out here," he said, cursing himself for sounding lame.

"Paradise," she said, tilting her head back. But there was a sad smile on her face.

"Where have you surfed?" he asked.

"California, Australia, here and there. This is my first time in Hawaii. I feel like the water calls to me." Michaela ducked her head, as if she hadn't meant to say that.

He knew what she meant and he wanted to know more. More about her surfing, more about her. "Do you want to go out to dinner with me tonight?"

For a minute, he didn't think she was going to answer him. Michaela frowned at the waves.

"I've got a beta version of the new Excel. I can show you my spreadsheets." He waggled his eyebrows at her. "We can concatenate"

That coaxed her smile back. "Yeah," she finally said. "I think I do."

Satisfaction was sweet. "What type of food do you like?"

"I always wanted to eat at Zippy's."

The smile froze on his face. Zippy's was a fast food restaurant. "Dear God, why?" came out of his mouth before he could stop it.

"The *ono grindz*, of course," she said.

"Don't listen to a word of what Makoa says when it comes to fine cuisine," Marcus warned.

"I'm on a mission to eat all of the malasadas on Maui."

It was a good goal. Those fried little doughnuts came in all shapes and flavors and when done right, melted in your mouth in a sugary explosion. "Maybe we could try another place?"

She shook her head. "Nah, never mind."

He missed seeing the next few waves while he was talking to Michaela, and he paddled up so he didn't lose his place. A few locals had pushed in front of him, but he didn't care. As he looked around the bay, Marcus could see the rest of the Palekaiko group heading in to shore. He wondered if they expected him to bring Michaela back with him. Marcus didn't mind, not by a long shot. Then it hit him what she said. "Wait, do you mean never mind on Zippy's or never mind on dinner?"

"Hey, try to get laid on your own time," the guy in back of him said. "You're out of turn." He pointed to Michaela.

"She's with me," Marcus said, his voice hard.

The guy squared off on him.

"That's fine. I wasn't going to cut in line. I was just talking," she said, with her hands up in a soothing manner.

"You here to surf or to talk?" the man sneered.

"Watch your tone," Marcus warned.

"No. No worries. I'm done for the day, anyway. Good luck," Michaela said, touching his leg.

Marcus glared at the man until he looked away, but Michaela had already left. He paddled up to get into position. He took a final glance back at Michaela. Fuck. Did he just blow it? She paddled away back towards the Palekaiko group where everyone was watching.

Great. No pressure.

The urge to show off was almost overwhelming. But he couldn't do aerials or any of the fancy new school surf tricks. But then again, he wasn't here to do anything but surf. Marcus was smart enough to realize he had a bigger chance of making an ass out of himself than he did looking like an ace. So in the end, he took a deep breath and cleared his mind of everything but the wind and the water.

The wave came in fast and he met it. Lifting up to his feet, Marcus dropped in the back door at the peak of the breaking wave.

Adrenaline surged through him as he balanced himself. The salt sprayed his face and he laughed. This was why he hadn't gone back to New York yet. Doing a bottom turn at the base of the wave, he carved his way through the water with crisp movements. Swaying with the ocean, he could almost believe his brother's bullshit philosophy.

"Tide goes in. Tide goes out. You can't control it. If you try, you'll get smashed by the ocean. Just got to go with the flow, brah."

Go with the flow.

Easier said than done.

Especially when the jackass from behind him, dropped in on his wave and cut him off. Then, he had the nerve to flip him off. Before he could think better of it, Marcus pushed off his own board, kicking it so it sailed in front of the man's path. Before Marcus hit the water himself, he saw the guy face plant in the water. The funny thing? Had the asshole been nice, Marcus would have let him go ahead of him in the line.

Maybe he needed to work on that inner peace thing a bit more.

Chapter Four

MICHAELA TURNED SO SHE COULD SEE MARCUS' ride. *Dayum*, he was a golden bronze god of a man. He was one of those surfers who made it look effortless. A stab of envy filled her at his flawless ride.

"*Kahuna* isn't bad," Hani said.

"Out here anyway," Joely laughed.

Michaela forced herself to look away before they caught her drooling at their boss. Zippy's had been a test. Gerald wouldn't have been caught dead in a place like that. She didn't need to go out with another Gerald, even if he was sex on a surfboard.

"He's a righteous prick on dry land," Kai added.

Then a surfer cut in front of him and they both wiped out.

Joely winced.

"Did he shoot his board at him?" Michaela asked. She was pretty sure she saw Marcus' board crash into the other man's.

"Not just on dry land," Hani said.

"We gotta head back," Makoa said.

"Especially since he caught us." Kai grimaced.

"You can use the board," Hani said to Michaela. "*Kahuna* can give you a ride back to the resort."

Panic warred with the desire to stay. As it was, she basically hitched a ride with strangers at six o'clock this morning to come here. Michaela had only been mildly reassured that they all worked at the resort she was staying in. And since the airline lost her luggage and still hadn't found it, she borrowed a wetsuit from

Joely and said, "What the heck?" But surfing with a billionaire hothead wasn't on her list of things to do today, no matter how tempting. She was done with high pressure men. Especially ones with tempers. If he had flicked his board at that jerk, that was dangerous.

"Nah, I'm about at my limit. I'll catch a ride back to the resort with you guys."

Hani looked a little disappointed. Michaela wondered if he was matchmaking. But they went in and hiked back to the van where they all piled back in again. She snoozed a bit against the window on the way back.

"See ya later, Michaela," Kai said, tossing off his shirt and hurrying to the lobby. Everyone else clambered out of the van and stretched.

"I got those," Makoa said, jerking his thumb at the boards. "I'll wipe 'em down and wax 'em up and maybe we can go again tomorrow."

"I'm on the early shift," Joely said with a face.

"Maybe," Michaela nodded.

"I'll check the *kahuna*'s schedule," Hani said. "Maybe tomorrow we'll go to the Dumps."

"Better you than me," Joely said. "They don't like me there."

"Why?" Michaela asked.

Hani rolled his eyes. "No one is going to say a word to you."

"It's a local spot," Joely said. "I'm nowhere near as good as they are." She indicated Hani and Kai with her hand as they walked through the lobby. Kai was at the front desk. He had combed his hair and was wearing a freshly ironed shirt that he must have had already prepped in a locker somewhere. He was on the phone and he appeared completely professional, not like he had spent the last four hours surfing rad waves. Michaela wondered if he was still in board shorts behind the desk.

"The first time I went, I got a lot of ribbing." Joely pointed to her strawberry blond hair. "So I was on a mission to prove myself. I wound up getting cut to shit on the reef. There was so much blood in the water that they were afraid of sharks." She showed her some scars on her arm.

Michaela winced.

"I haven't lived that down yet."

"Holt won't let them say a word to you," Hani said.

Joely's face flamed red to the tips of her ears. "Holt didn't speak to me for a week after that happened." Joely shuddered. "He thinks I'm an idiot," she whispered.

"Who's Holt?" Michaela asked.

"He's the head of security here," Joely said.

"And Marcus' right hand man. See you guys later." Hani ducked into the resort shop.

She and Joely walked back towards the rooms together. "He's one of those strict, but fair guys. I think he has some sort of mysterious past."

"What do you mean?" Michaela liked the harmless gossip. In her law firm she was "the man" and she was sure her paralegal chatted about her and Gerald when Michaela wasn't around.

"I don't know. I heard he's got some military background. He doesn't talk much about himself. And I've never seen him even touch a drink, so he's usually the designated driver when he can be convinced to go out."

"Does Marcus or his brother ever hang with the staff?"

"When Amelia can drag them. They're not so bad, as far as bosses go. Dude is happy as long as he has beer, and Amelia takes time out of her day to hang with him."

"What makes Marcus happy?" Michaela wondered.

Joely shrugged. "Profit margin?"

They giggled.

As they came up to the staff quarters, Joely said, "I'm sure the airport will have your luggage to us by lunch."

"Oh that reminds me," Michaela said, veering off to the laundry room. "I've got to pick up my clothes. I'll wash your wetsuit."

"No worries," Joely said. "Just fold it up and I'll grab it when I clean your room."

"Thanks again for letting me tag along."

"Did you have fun?"

Michaela nodded. "I really did." They made her feel like she was one of the group instead of the odd girl out. It was like hanging out with friends. Actually, better. The last time she and Gerald had entertained, they had wine and hors d'oeuvres with friends and wound up talking about politics and law for the whole night. It was like Michaela had forgotten what it was like to have fun.

"Thanks again," she said.

Joely gave her the shaka and headed over to where the staff lived. Michaela thought it was a pretty sweet deal. They got room and board, in addition to their salary. Joely said the only thing they had to pay for was booze.

After collecting her outfit from the dryer, Michaela climbed the three floors to her room. When she got to the landing, she had to push aside a heavy plastic tarp and weave around tools and sawhorses. She saw that the workman had started to install the electronic locks, but for the moment her big key hanging from a plumeria Shrinky Dink keychain still opened her door.

Stepping carefully over the bare wood of the floor, she made a bee line to her phone. It should be fully charged now. Turning it on, Michaela braced herself for the incoming messages. But there weren't any.

Do I not have any signal?

Nope. Full bars.

That didn't make sense. Not one call from her parents, her friends, her company? And, of course, not one from Gerald either. She dialed her office. It would be around four in the afternoon there.

The receptionist picked up on the first ring. "Kennedy law firm, how many I direct your call?"

"Hi Jean, can I speak to Gayle?"

"Who's calling, please?"

Michaela looked at the phone. "Jean, it's me. Michaela."

"Oh," she said. "Oh." There was a long pause and then another. "Oh."

"Is she in?" Michaela said slowly, wondering what all the "ohs" meant.

"Yes. Hold please."

Their hold music was the local radio station and Michaela smirked at the traffic report, glad she wasn't planning to drive in that today.

"Attorney Harris," Gayle said. "Where are you?"

Michaela frowned. Jeez, that was abrupt. Her paralegal wasn't her best friend, but they were friendly. Gayle could have asked how she was doing, at least. She knew she was supposed to have gotten married this week. Michaela wasn't naïve enough to think the news about Gerald flaking out on her didn't get back to the office, but she still had expected some chit chat.

"I'm on vacation," Michaela said. "Where did you think I was?"

"Well, everyone thought you'd be in today. We were getting worried."

"Not worried enough to call me," Michaela said, forcing a calm she didn't feel. Was that why no one was blowing up her phone? Did they think she was sulking in her condo?

"Attorney Rivers wanted to speak to you as soon as you checked in. I can transfer you over to him now."

"Hold on a second," she said, and then paused. Michaela had just been about to ask Gayle to grab her spare key from her desk and go to her house and Fed Ex her laptop to Maui. But on second thought maybe she should hear what her boss, the senior partner, had to say.

Rooting around in her purse, Michaela found an unopened vodka nip that the flight attendant comped her once she told her what happened. "Okay, go ahead."

She took a swig just as Tim Rivers came on the phone.

"Michaela, how are you holding up?" His voice was full of professional sympathy.

"I'm pissed, but it's nothing two weeks of surf, sand, and . . ." she almost said sex as a picture of Marcus floated through her mind. Where the hell did that come from? "Sunshine won't fix,"

Michaela substituted. She put the little vodka bottle down before it loosened her tongue even more.

"We hadn't expected you to still take your vacation."

"Why not?"

"Well," he drew out the word and she figured he was trying to think of a tactful way to mention that she wasn't on her honeymoon. "I figured you would want to save this time for later this year when you and Gerald reschedule the wedding."

Michaela barked out a laugh that was probably too loud. "There isn't going to be a wedding. I don't know what you heard, but Gerald decided to call it off at the last minute."

"I understand he had cold feet. It happens."

Spoken like a true lawyer.

"But I'm sure once he thinks about it, he'll realize what a good match you two are, both personally and professionally."

"Too little. Too late. Look, there's a sunburn that's waiting on me. If there isn't anything else…?" Michaela was not in the mood to deal with this shit.

"So you're not still in California?"

"No," Michaela said. "I'm in Hawaii."

"But Gerald cancelled your plans."

Michaela almost choked on air. "Well, at least he told you that. I haven't heard from the son of a bitch."

"Oh."

Here we go with the "Ohs" again. Michaela rolled her eyes. "I'll see you in two weeks. My plans haven't changed."

"I see," he said, not sounding too convinced of that. "I had you on the schedule for some research and I needed you to go to court on Thursday to fill in. I don't suppose you could cut your vacation short?"

"No. I can't," Michaela said and then added, "Sorry."

Not sorry.

"But you're all alone."

Thanks for pointing that out.

"Actually with all due respect, who I'm with or not with is really none of your business."

"I see," he said, coldly.

"*Aloha*, Tim." She ended the call. She might have just sabotaged her road to partnership with that conversation.

Do I give a fuck?

Not at the moment. Michaela would probably regret it once she was back on the mainland. But for right now, she was still riding high on the waves, drinking vodka before lunch and thinking about kissing a hothead billionaire who was snobby about food.

Typical Monday, right?

What she wouldn't give for a handset and a receiver so she could slam the phone down. Michaela thought about giving Gerald a piece of her mind, but forced herself to hide her phone in the rickety bureau. Out of sight. Out of mind.

She would not call him first. He owed her an explanation, but she would be damned if she would beg for one.

Quiet knocking on her door caught Michaela's attention and she peeked through the peephole.

"Hi Amelia," she said and let her in. "I haven't had time to get my thoughts together on the Honolua Bay trip. But off the top of my head, I think it would be a great snorkeling adventure when the weather is calm. But for a surfing excursion, it would be a little dangerous."

"Oh," Amelia said.

Here we go with the "ohs" again.

Amelia shook her head and said, "Thanks for that. But that's not why I'm here. It's a little embarrassing." She shifted from one foot to the other. "There's a bit of a hitch in our situation."

Folding her arms, Michaela rested her hip on the bureau. "Story of my life, lately. What's up?" She drained the vodka and tossed the bottle into the trash can with a satisfying thunk.

"Technically, you can't be here, right?" Amelia fidgeted.

Michaela nodded. "Yeah, I figured it was some sort of safety hazard."

"So you can't let anyone know you're here."

"Too late. I went surfing this morning with half of your staff."

Amelia waved her hand. "No, not them. I'm not worried about them. I'm worried about Marcus."

"Oh," Michaela said. The "Ohs" must be catching.

"Marcus is a good guy. He's wrapped a little tight, and gets bogged down with the details."

"I know the type. I almost married one."

Amelia chewed on her lip. "Anyway, I got a call this morning from a local pain in the ass. Long story short, Tetsuo and I have a history of antagonizing each other. Marcus and Samuel are the current owners of the resort, but Tetsuo wasn't happy about selling it to them last year. But he had made a promise and felt honor bound to keep it. However, it hasn't stopped him from looking for ways to shut us down."

Michaela wasn't sure she followed Amelia's train of thought. "So what does that have to do with Marcus not knowing I'm squatting here until a room comes available?"

"Tetsuo would like nothing more for than to see the resort fail, so he can buy it up again and plow it into the sand to build condos. One way to do that is to get our housing permits revoked. Or keep the inspectors on our ass until we get fed up and sell."

"So, do you want me to leave?" Michaela didn't think she could take another blow.

"No, no."

She sagged in relief.

"Just don't tell Marcus that you're staying here. He's a little freaked out because we got sanctioned for holding weddings on the beach."

"What the heck is wrong with that?" It seemed like the perfect place to have a wedding. Maybe next time…Who was she kidding? There wasn't going to be a next time.

Amelia rolled her eyes. "Apparently, the beach is a public place and it's illegal to get married on public property without a permit and without heavy restrictions. I might have bent the rules and we got slammed for it. So we have a few black marks against us in the Chamber of Commerce for that and we've had to pay a shit ton of fines."

"Sounds like you might need a lawyer." The wheels in Michaela's head were turning. If she could bum a computer, she might be able to do some research for Amelia. Or maybe she could take a taxi to the local library. She should probably hit the Walmart too, just in case her luggage didn't get here for a few more days.

Amelia grimaced. "Marcus hates lawyers."

Well, that figured.

"I'm an attorney," Michaela said.

"Oh," Amelia gasped and clapped a hand to her mouth. "I'm glad I didn't do a shark joke."

"Go ahead. I've heard them all," Michaela said. "Let me guess, something about a shark not attacking a lawyer because of professional courtesy?"

"Not even a little bit original, huh?" Amelia winced. "Well, it doesn't help that we tried hiring a local attorney and got the runaround, so we hired a mainland firm and they've been dicking us around just as hard. So lawyers are a touchy subject around here."

"It's okay. All right, I'll lay low and avoid Marcus." Well, shit. She had almost decided to keep at him until he took her to Zippy's, even if it was against her better judgment.

"You don't have to avoid him. Just don't tell him where you're staying. You should, however, avoid the security chief. His name is Holt Tanaka and he'll snitch to Marcus. If he even gets wind you might be up to something, he'll be on you like white on rice. He's excellent at his job, but someone needs to dislodge the stick in his ass." Amelia sighed.

"Joely mentioned him." Michaela wondered if she'd have to sneak around like a ninja at night. "What about your husband? Won't he be mad at you when he finds out you're bending the rules for me?"

Amelia snorted. "He's the least of your worries. He couldn't care less. I think he'd be secretly relieved if he was forced to shut down the resort and sell it back to Tetsuo. It's too much responsibility for him. I can't tell him either about this because he'll also tattle to Marcus, and Marcus will make me kick you out.

As far as I'm concerned for the Kincaide brothers, it's out of sight out of mind."

"Got it. I won't do anything to call attention to myself." That shouldn't be a problem. Michaela was only going to be in her room for showering and sleeping.

"If you want to meet Dude, he's in a hammock on the beach between two stone palm trees. If you want snorkeling lessons, tell him I comped you."

"I know how to snorkel. Can I get gear from him?"

She nodded and headed for the door. "Yup, the gear rental's on me."

"I really appreciate that," Michaela said.

"It's the least I can do. Don't worry, as soon as we have an open suite, I'll send Makoa and the boys over to help you with your stuff."

"What stuff?" Michaela indicated the empty room.

"Oh yeah. If you give me the airline's information, I can harass them for your luggage."

"You don't mind? I was going to do that next."

"Yeah, not a problem. You go stroll around and maybe sample some of the local waves. They're nothing like Honolua, but the beach is all sand. No rocks or coral. Watch out for the current, though, especially around Black Rock."

"Thanks, I'll probably head over there after lunch. And don't worry. I'll keep your secret. I don't want you guys to get into trouble."

Chapter Five

THERE WAS A LULL IN THE WAVES and the wind changed. Based on the grumbling, Marcus didn't think there would be anymore big waves for a while. Time to go back and grill Hani about Michaela. He never did get her number, but he wasn't going to give up on dinner. Even if it did mean a dinner of breaded mahi and fries at Zippy's.

But when he got back to Palekaiko, no one was in the lobby or at the desk.

"For fuck's sake," Marcus growled and stormed out into the courtyard.

All the vendor's tables were empty too and some chairs were knocked over. That wasn't good. His first thought was, "What had Tetsuo done now?" But then Marcus heard the screams from the beach and he broke out into a run.

In the ocean, he saw Samuel's Zodiac zooming in towards the beach, overloaded with people. Out of the corner of his eye, Makoa, Hani and Kai were running down the beach with another inflatable boat.

"What's going on?" he asked, catching up to them.

"Shark attacked a guy kite surfing, and everyone's panicking," Kai said.

"Is he all right?"

"One bite and the shark spit him out, but he was in shock. They think he might lose his arm. The ambulance just left." Kai jumped in the boat and Marcus helped push him into the water.

Squinting out into the waves, Marcus didn't see any fins. He waded up to where Samuel had beached his boat and helped people out of the water.

"Where's Amelia?" Marcus asked him.

"Meeting with DLNR and the other hotel managers."

His brother wore sunglasses and a ball cap. He had on neon board shorts. His shaggy blond hair hung to his shoulders and he looked like a dirt bag. But he got the kids in the boat with him to laugh and they gave him fast shakas as they ran up the beach to go jump into the pool.

Marcus wished he could bounce back that quickly. His heart was still pounding, and he was out of breath. The Department of Land and Natural Resources would close down the beach until tomorrow at least. And after inspection, they'd probably give the all clear before noon. Sharks happen. But tell that to the guy who just got chomped.

"Tetsuo is with them," Samuel said.

Marcus snorted. "Did he bring the shark?"

"I wouldn't put it past him."

Kai was on his way back in with a full boat. It looked like they got everyone on their stretch of beach, except for a chick in a white bikini on a long board. His brain short circuited when he realized it was Michaela. Instead of body boarding in, like a sane person would, she was paddling further out.

"What does that *lolo* think she's doing?" Samuel said.

Marcus scanned for a fin, but even though he didn't see one, he grew cold and started dragging the boat. "Help me get this thing back in the water. I'll go get her."

Michaela was kneeling on the board, hunched over. She was heading for something.

"All right. Got a cold beer with your name on it when you come back." They tugged the Zodiac out and Marcus jumped in.

"I might need something stronger."

He set the outboard and rode out as fast as he could. Before he could shout to Michaela, he saw the kid. Holy shit, how did they miss him? As he got closer, she helped the boy on the board with her. She swayed as his long legs almost knocked her in the water, but she held steady on the board. The kid was about fifteen and had on a snorkel and mask. Where the crap were his parents?

"Get in," he said, pulling the small boat beside them.

"Wait," Michaela said, as the teenager lunged off the board and scrambled into the Zodiac. Michaela flipped over and landed in the water.

Marcus' arm shot out and grabbed her. He hauled her up and over into the boat. She flopped across his lap. It wasn't graceful. It wasn't pretty, but no limbs were in the water. Her surfboard was still leashed to her ankle, so it trailed behind them as they headed for the beach.

"Thanks for saving me, man," the kid said. "I didn't know what was going on. I was underwater throughout all of it."

"Did you see the shark?"

"No," he groaned in disappointment.

Michaela hadn't moved from being sprawled over him. He was uncomfortably aware of how smooth her skin was and how very little the triangle swatch of fabric over her ass covered.

"You okay?" Marcus asked her.

"Michaela is not in right now. Please leave a message and she'll get back to you shortly," she muttered, her face buried in the side of the boat.

"All right, then." He patted her back.

Samuel was waiting for him with the rest of the crew and they pulled the boat up to the beach. The kid jumped out.

"Thanks again," he called as he headed down the beach towards the time shares.

"Dry land," Marcus said and helped Michaela to her feet. Hani slipped the surf board's leash off her foot.

"How were the waves?" Hani asked.

"Not now," Marcus said, holding Michaela up when her knees jiggled. "I'm going to need your hammock," he said to his brother.

"*K'den*," Samuel said, eyeballing the two of them.

Marcus hooked his arm around Michaela's waist and half carried her up to the hammock.

She wrapped her arms around him and hugged so tight, he could barely breathe, but who needed air anyway? "You should lie down." He tried to disengage her arms.

She wouldn't budge.

"Okay. I'm going to lie down and take you with me." Easing himself into the wide hammock, Marcus laid down. Michaela immediately snuggled in next to him.

With the soft breeze and the bright sun, he could almost see why his brother chose to spend his days swinging on the hammock and drinking beer.

"So this is awkward," she said, her face buried in his chest.

"You're right. I don't think we've been formally introduced. I'm Marcus Kincaide from New York. I own a chain of hotels there, and one here in Maui."

"Michaela Harris," she whispered. "I surf in shark infested waters and laugh in the face of danger."

"Laugh?"

"More of a whimper, actually."

"I think you're very brave." He smoothed his hand over her hair. It was pulled back into a pony tail, and he itched to undo it to see her hair fanned out over her back. "So now that we've been introduced, it's no longer awkward."

She laughed against his chest. "I'll let you go in a few minutes."

"No hurry," he said, and tucked a few stray strands of hair behind her ear. As long as her leg didn't move up a few inches, he could hide his growing hard on. She felt like she belonged in his arms.

"Isn't your brother going to want his hammock back?" she mumbled.

"Fuck him." And for good measure, Marcus gave Samuel the bird as he walked by. Not one to miss a witty rejoinder, Samuel grabbed his balls and mouthed, "Blow me."

"So, how was *your* day?" she asked.

He told her about the rest of the waves at Honolua Bay and how he caught four more. All in all, it was a good day of surfing. As he droned on about the details of the waves and what each surfer did, her body slowly unclenched and relaxed against his. He, however, was sweating and it had nothing to do with the sun. He was well aware all he had to do was pull on the string and her top would be undone.

"I saw the fin," she said, pushing up into a seated position.

Marcus grabbed one of his brother's ball caps that he had lying around, and strategically placed it in his lap.

"How far away was it?" he asked, stroking her arm because he couldn't help himself. Her skin was flawless.

"Far enough that I convinced myself I could body surf back to shore. But when I looked back to see if it decided to follow me, I saw the kid's snorkel tube."

"So you turned back around?" That took serious balls.

"You would have done the same. What was I supposed to do, scream for help? I was right there."

"Where was the shark?"

Michaela shrugged. "Who knows? He could have been right there or he could have swam away."

"What happened to the kite surfer?" Marcus knew that sharks were a matter of course. While attacks were more common on Maui, it wasn't a daily or even a weekly occurrence.

"I didn't see it, but I think the shark took a bite out of him and his rig."

"So there was blood in the water?"

Michaela nodded. "Had to be. So more sharks could have been coming to investigate." She thunked him on his chest. "Thanks for that. I was just beginning to calm down."

"You handled yourself great." He reached over to his brother's cooler and pulled out two Coronas. He handed them to her. "I think the opener is on the palm tree."

"It's not my first time swimming with a shark." When she stood up and opened the beers, he took the time to admire her long legs. "But I have to say, this time was the scariest. The last few times I was closer to shore and wasn't trying to rescue anyone but myself." Michaela tossed the caps in the trash and came back to sit next to him on the hammock.

"Brave and beautiful," he said, moving over to give her a little more room.

She shrugged, but a tiny smile crossed her face. She handed a beer back to him.

"Let me take you out to dinner," he said. "I know it's no Zippy's, but there's a great restaurant down the beach called Leilani's. After all this excitement, I figured you could use a nice bottle of wine and some *ono grindz*." He mimicked her pidgin from this afternoon.

"You rescued me. Maybe I should be buying you dinner." She took a healthy gulp of the cold beer.

"Okay," he said. "I'm easy. As long as we have a date tonight."

"A date?" She tilted her head and looked at him assessingly.

"Unless you have a boyfriend."

"Not anymore," she said. "I got dumped a few days ago."

"The man's an idiot," Marcus said, and then realized he said that aloud.

Michaela nodded. "I'm beginning to think so."

"So where can I pick you up?"

She shifted her eyes away. "Just tell me where and when and I'll meet you."

Hmm, she was cautious. He had to work on getting her to trust him. It was hard to think, though, sitting so close to her when she had on that little bikini. Marcus forced his eyes up to her pretty face instead of the soft curves that had just been pressed up against him. He drained his beer to try and cool off.

Michaela's heartbeat was finally back to normal, but she still wanted to lie back down into Marcus' arms. How long had it been since she cuddled with a warm body? Too long. And certainly not with a muscled surfer, not since high school at least. Her eyes traced the line of hair that went from his abs to his belly button. His board shorts were slung low so she could just see the V handles on his hips. What were those called? Obliques? No, the Adonis belt. She grinned. That certainly was a fitting description. Michaela resisted the urge to jump back on top of him.

"So how about you? Is there a girlfriend hanging around the beach looking to drown me?" she asked.

"Nope."

"Why the hell not?" Michaela asked, and then realized she said that aloud.

He stretched and she admired the flex of muscles. Unable to stop herself, she placed her hand on his chest. His gaze went molten as they locked eyes.

"I caught my fiancée bent over her desk by her paralegal."

Michaela snatched her hand back. "That's awful." His cheating fiancée had been a lawyer. No wonder he hated attorneys.

He reclaimed her hand and brought it to his lips for a kiss. It was charming and sexy all at the same time. "Better than waiting until after the wedding to find out."

"You got that right," she huffed.

Marcus sat up, his legs straddling the hammock. His knee brushed her thigh and she realized she was seriously considering kissing him.

It was supposed to be her honeymoon after all.

"She had told me she was going to be working long hours on her case. She was a prosecutor on Long Island. I drove in from the city to surprise her with dinner in her office." Marcus gave a half laugh. "I surprised her all right."

"I'm sorry," Michaela said. At least she had been spared that from Gerald. "How long ago?" She could still hear the pain in his voice.

"Two years." He shrugged.

"You must have loved her very much."

"It was a good match."

She cringed. That sounded too familiar. "Why did you ask her to marry you if you didn't love her?" When she heard the anger in her voice, she realized she wasn't really asking Marcus that question. "Sorry," she sighed shakily. "None of my business." She looked out into the ocean and wondered if the shark would put her out of her misery.

Damn it, she didn't want to still be hurt by Gerald's fuckery.

"It's a valid question." He stared over her head, lost in thought. "I guess I thought it was time to get married. We were compatible. I liked her and she liked me. Our families got along."

Each word was like a punch to her gut. She took another gulp of her beer.

"I hated that she cheated on me, but was worse was she lied to me. I felt like a fool."

Michaela could relate to that. "She should have been honest with you and told you she wanted to marry for love."

"She still wanted to marry me," Marcus scoffed.

Michaela's head whipped back to him. "What?"

"She was *screwing* her secretary. She wanted to *marry* me. I had money and prestige. She had it all figured out. Fucking lawyers. I hate them."

Story of her life.

"Why wasn't she fucking you instead?" Michaela clamped a hand over her mouth. "Sorry. I'm not sure where the hell my filters are today."

"She was. It wasn't like we were too busy for each other. We went at it like rabbits just the night before."

Michaela was officially mortified. More beer. That had to be the solution. She took another swig. "So did she apologize for having the affair and swore to never do it again?"

He barked out a half laugh. "No, she suggested that we have an open marriage. We'd be a power couple to the media and at parties, but if one of us wanted to indulge in an affair, then why not? She made a good argument."

"Lawyers usually do," Michaela said lightly.

"Hey, why did the shark..."

"Professional courtesy." She considered dumping the rest of her beer over his head.

"She could debate circles around me. It was sometimes just easier to give in, than to make everything a court room battle."

"Why didn't you go for it? It sounds like the perfect arrangement for any guy. All the sex you want, and none of the guilt."

Is that what Gerald had wanted, but was smart enough not to suggest that to her? Suddenly, she wanted to check Facebook and see if his ex girlfriend was still with her bass player.

"Because I don't share what's mine."

His tone had her snapping her attention back to him. Very caveman of him. She liked it. Digging her toes in the sand, she asked, "Why aren't you with anyone if it's been two years?"

"It's easier to just have short term relationships. Hot, intense, and over before anyone can get hurt."

He made a good point.

"Must get awfully lonely," she said, sipping from her beer bottle.

"Just the opposite."

She smiled without humor. Yeah, he probably didn't have a hard time finding women to keep him company.

Michaela wanted to touch him. Her fingers itched to stroke his thigh, but a part of her was afraid of pulling on the tiger's tail. The way he was looking at her left little doubt that he would be ready and willing to escalate the situation. Short, hot, intense. No strings.

That so wasn't her. But maybe it could be. Just for a few days.

"I work a lot. So I don't really have time to put into a relationship."

"You get out what you put in," she said.

"Roger dat," he said with feeling and winked at her.

She groaned. "Not what I meant."

Michaela should go before she got herself into trouble. The temptation was huge to rebound right into Marcus' arms. Hell, she had spent a good hour in them already. Her body wanted more of his hard muscles under her fingers and the soft cushion of his chest when she rested her head there. But she had never before slept with a man so soon after meeting him. Michaela wasn't even sure she could. Then again, what else did she need to know about him? Boozy sex was what she had been looking forward to. Why not indulge in a vacation affair?

"I've been meaning to get back to my life in New York, but I can't quite bring myself to do it. I can be more efficient on the East Coast. Amelia can handle everything here, as long as Samuel grows the hell up. Sometimes, I think I'm missing out on something obvious and that's why I'm here." He gave a half laugh. "Amelia's aunt is a fortune teller. She sets up a table with the rest of the craft vendors on Thursday, but sometimes you'll catch her around. She likes to read my cards."

"What does she say?"

"The same cryptic crap that they all do. My destiny is in my own hands and I need to be patient." He rolled his eyes. "I don't do patient. She tells me that I need to learn to lighten up and relax, that my temper will be the means to my doom" Marcus dragged out the last word in a deep ominous tone. "Frankly, I think Samuel tips her a twenty just to say those things."

"I'll have to look her up. I've had a major upheaval in my life I could use some guidance from the great beyond."

His phone rang.

"Shit," he said. "I forgot I had that in my pocket when I went out to get you."

Michaela didn't want to have him answer that and leave her sitting there awkwardly. Taking a deep breath, she was about to get up when he switched off the phone.

She blinked at him in surprise.

"How did it end with your man?" he asked.

Did she want to tell him? Admit how pathetic she was. She shook her head. But he shut off his phone for her. Gerald never would have. The last thing she wanted was his pity, though, so she kept it vague.

"He stopped calling. I got the message."

It wasn't a total lie.

"Good," he said.

"Good?" Michaela wasn't expecting that response, but before she could follow up with a question, Marcus cupped the back of her head and kissed her. The beer bottle dropped from her nerveless fingers.

She rested her hand on his shoulder, only briefly considering shoving him back. But his mouth was soft and sweet and the dip of his tongue made her dizzy and hungry for him. Maybe a temporary thing was just what she needed to get some confidence back.

Marcus laid back down in the hammock, pulling her with him so she rested on top of him. His erection pressed into her stomach.

Oh, hell yes.

She entangled her legs with his and wrapped her arms around his neck. Michaela wasn't sure how long they kissed, but it was sooner than she was ready to be interrupted, when someone cleared his throat a few times.

She broke away, embarrassed to see a man who looked like a bigger version of Matthew McConaughey standing over them.

"No *puinsai* in my hammock," he said.

"Fuck off," Marcus snarled and went to kiss her again, but she stood up in a hurry.

"Hi," she said. "You must be Dude." She held out her hand, but he didn't shake it. His arms were crossed over his barrel chest and he glared down at his brother.

"What crawled up your ass?" Marcus asked, getting up.

"Tetsuo Hojo. He's accusing us of having panhandlers on the property, bothering the guests."

"That's bullshit. Where's Amelia?"

"She's handling him. I had to leave before I punched him out. He says we've got squatters camping out on the beach as well."

Michaela's heart dropped into her feet. She hoped she wasn't getting Amelia in trouble.

"I'll straighten him out." Marcus grabbed a shirt and pulled it on over his head.

That was her cue to leave. She wasn't sure where she was going, but it wasn't back to her room just yet. She headed down the beach towards the time shares. If she cut through them, she might be able to sneak back on the property to her room without anyone seeing her.

It wasn't until she made it back unseen and collapsed on her bed, that she realized he left her again without a second glance.

Swell.

Chapter Six

MICHAELA WAS HAVING A REALLY SEXY dream about tracing Marcus' Adonis belt with her tongue when her fucking cell phone woke her up.

"What?" She answered it without thinking. If this was Gerald, there was no way she could have this conversation without a pot of coffee spiked with Kahlúa.

"Hi Mrs. Stone, this is Paradise Airlines. I wanted to let you know that we've located your suitcase and it's in a taxi on its way to you."

"Um..." Michaela sat up. "What time is it?"

"It's just after nine a.m."

Which was six a.m. for Michaela. Too early for this shit.

"Your bag should be on your doorstep by noon."

That hit her like snorting coffee grounds.

"What? Where are you sending my luggage?"

"To seventeen Prince Street in Malibu," the woman said with a hint of attitude in her voice.

Get snotty with me, will you?

"I'm in fucking Maui. Why are you delivering my bag to my home? I'm not there."

She gave a nervous giggle. "Well, you see Mrs. Stone..."

"Harris," Michaela barked. "Attorney Harris."

"Oh. I have you down as..."

"I don't care."

"Your bag never left Los Angeles," she finished, quickly before Michaela could interrupt her.

"Listen to me," Michaela ran her fingers through her hair in frustration. "No one will be there to pick up my bag. It will sit on my step until someone steals it. I need you to bring it back to the airport and this time put it on a fucking plane to Maui, like I paid you the ridiculous fee of twenty-five bucks to do."

"I'm afraid I can't do that."

"What?" Michaela wiped the sleep out of her eyes. "Why not?"

"The taxi is already gone."

"Call him."

"I don't have his number," the woman said.

Michaela resisted the urge to scream. "Put me on hold. Call the taxi company and have them call the driver." Why was she telling this woman her job? Oh right, because they were about to drop a three thousand dollar bag on her doorstep. Which would be a huge flag to whomever steals it that Michaela wasn't home.

The woman came back on the line. "I'm sorry Miss Harris. The driver isn't answering his cell phone. Of course, we'll refund you the baggage fee."

"Great. Just great." Michaela hung up.

What the hell was she going to do? She couldn't call Gayle and have her wait at her condo until the luggage appeared. It was one thing to ask her to do a quick errand, but with the way traffic was who knew when her bag was going to get there? She had pissed off her boss enough this week without dragging a paralegal out of the office for most of the day.

Michaela called her mother. It went to voice mail. She was probably still sleeping, the phone turned off so as not to disturb her beauty rest. She hung up without leaving a message and tried her father. Also voice mail. He was probably chewing someone a new asshole and chomping antacids like they were M&Ms.

Gerald was the only one else who had a key to her condo.

"Damn it to hell." For a moment, she considered writing off the suitcase and everything in it. Then she thought of all the cute outfits she bought and the expensive lingerie inside her designer suitcase. "Shit."

Michaela dialed Gerald, hoping for voice mail. So naturally, he answered on the first ring.

"Michaela, I'm so glad you called."

Rage choked her. He sounded normal and pleasant, as if nothing had happened. "Look," she said. "I need you to go to my condo and wait for the taxi driver to deliver my suitcase. LAX never put it on the plane and instead of sending it to me, they decided to drive it home instead."

"I can't," he said, with just enough of regret in his voice to drive her bat shit. "I've got a busy schedule today."

"Can you send someone?" she said through her teeth. She didn't give a crap if he wasted *his* admin's time.

"Why don't you come home? I miss you."

Michaela had to clamp her hand over her mouth before she started screaming obscenities at him. Was he that clueless? He didn't even bother to explain why he never went to the church. He was just going to pretend that nothing had ever happened. Just a typical Wednesday.

"Are you there?" he asked when the silence between them grew uncomfortable for him.

She decided to avoid his misdirection and concentrate on the real reason why she called. He didn't show up at the church because he was an asshole. They didn't have a relationship because they didn't love each other, and a friend wouldn't have humiliated her like that.

"Can you rescue my bag or do I have to write that off as a loss as well?" It was tough to keep the bitterness out of her voice.

"I think I can send an intern. Do you mind if a stranger is in your house?"

"No. I just don't want to lose all my clothes and my Louis Vuitton suitcase."

"Hold for a moment and I'll see what I can do."

Flopping back on the bed, Michaela listened to the insipid Muzak. She was pretty sure it was AC/DC's *Hell's Bells*. What was she going to do if he couldn't find anyone to watch for her bag? Should she just admit defeat and go back home? She was alone, without a computer or a decent change of clothes, and she didn't even have an official hotel room. If she caught a plane now, there was a chance she'd be back home before dark and her suitcase might still be there.

"Darling?" he said when he got back on the line.

Go fuck yourself.

That was almost out before she caught herself. "Can your intern wait at my condo until the taxi with my bag gets there?" she asked instead.

"Not a problem."

Finally, something went right.

"I was thinking maybe I could bring it to you this weekend."

"What?" Michaela sat bolt upright.

"We'd still have a week's vacation together."

"Go fuck yourself." There was no stopping it this time.

"I understand you're upset, but this isn't a deal breaker for us."

"Go fuck yourself." It was louder this time. Not a deal breaker? The only thing that would have been worse would have been if he had been banging his ex-girlfriend in the vestibule before the ceremony.

"I made a mistake," Gerald's voice was showing the slightest bit of aggravation. "I'm sorry you're upset."

Not, I'm sorry I changed my mind about getting married.

Not, I'm sorry I humiliated you.

Not, I'm sorry I haven't called to explain.

Gerald continued, oblivious to the fact she was seething with fury at him. "I had a lot of pressure from a few clients, and I needed to be in a different frame of mind before I could marry you. I just needed a few days to clear my head and concentrate on work. I was able to close a few cases and get a head start on some research, so now I can enjoy my vacation."

"Fuck you!" She hung up on him and stalked over to her carry-on. Taking the ring box out, Michaela flung it as hard as she could at the wall. It bounced off and tumbled close to her. She picked it up and hurled it at the wall twice more. Then stomped on it for good measure.

Her phone rang, but she ignored it. When it was clear that Gerald wasn't going to stop calling, Michaela turned the phone off and stuffed it in the drawer.

She practiced her deep breathing exercises in the shower, but she was still pissed off. Luckily, her bikini was dry because she needed to get into the water, right now, and let the waves pound the anger out of her. However when she got down to the beach, the shark warning signs were still out.

"Figures," she said. But even though she was mad enough to take on a shark, she knew there were other beaches that were safe for her to swim out her anger on.

As she strode into the lobby, she was surprised to see Marcus at his computer in one of the large wicker chairs. He didn't look up, and she didn't think she could handle another workaholic asshole, so she didn't interrupt him.

"*Howzit*," Michaela said to Makoa who was behind the tour excursion desk.

"Hey, girl. You ready to go back in the water?"

"*Shoots.*" She grinned, feeling a little better after using some of the slang they taught her yesterday. "Have you seen Hani?"

"It's his day off. He's probably home. Want me to call him?"

"That won't be necessary," Marcus said.

Michaela jumped. She hadn't heard him come up behind her. She gave him a tight smile. His eyes narrowed on her. "Are you all right?"

"Fine," she said. "No. Not fine. I need to surf. The rougher the waves, the better."

"Do you want some company? It's not a good idea to surf alone, even if you wouldn't be alone for long, especially in that bikini."

She smiled at that. He was good at flirting. "Sure, if you can fit it in with your busy schedule."

"For you and that suit, I'd make time," he said.

Really good at flirting.

Then he walked away from her again.

Well, fuck him too.

Except, he came back with his laptop closed. "Let's go."

"Uh, this is kind of embarrassing," she said. "I need to borrow a board."

"Not a problem. Are you sure you want to surf in that?" He gave her a slow once over that shouldn't have made her toes curl, but it did.

"You got a problem with my suit?" She put her hands on her hips. A part of her recognized that she was looking for a fight, but she ignored the caution signs. She probably should just put her travel clothes back on and take a cab to Walmart, but she didn't want to waste the waves. She actually had wanted to buy a wetsuit of her own today, so she didn't have to keep borrowing Joely's, but Gerald's asshattery blew all of her plans out of the water.

"Nope, I'm a big fan of that suit." Marcus slung an arm around her waist and steered her out into the courtyard.

Michaela wanted to calm down enough to have a conversation with him, but she was still stewing over Gerald. Marcus' body was nice and warm, and it felt so damn good to be held. Her anger was turning into something else entirely, and she put her arm around him as well.

She couldn't help remembering how nice he was yesterday when she needed comfort. "I wanted to thank you for getting me out of the ocean fast."

"My pleasure," he said, pulling her in to kiss her temple. "I'm sorry I had to leave before we were able to finish what we started.

Michaela knew her faced flamed up. "It's probably good your brother showed up when he did."

"It's never good when he shows up. Trust me on that." He laughed.

"Where are we going?" she asked, leaning her head against him. Her angry stride was slowly turning into a leisurely saunter.

"I've got to change and grab my boards. Are you hungry?"

"Yeah," she admitted.

He pulled out his cell phone, and she glared at him until she realized he was ordering breakfast for them. "Hi Pololena, can you send up two cheese omelets and toast, a pot of coffee and fruit salad?" Marcus moved the phone away from his mouth. "Anything else?"

Normally, she would have gotten pissed about him ordering for her, but it felt comforting, like he was taking care of her. Her rage lowered a peg and simmered into the awareness that had flared between them yesterday.

"No thanks," she said. "That all sounds wonderful."

He slipped his phone back into his pants. "I was thinking we could go to Ho'okipa. It's got some long rides. It looks like you could use that."

"Yeah." Michaela hugged him. He understood. "Are you sure you don't have to work?"

"I'm sure that I want to spend time with you more that I want to work," he said.

That pleased her more than it should. Finally, someone who put her first. "I'd like that too."

He led her to one of the buildings that were close to the water, and they took the elevator all the way up to the top floor.

It opened up into a short hallway. "There's only three suites up here. Samuel and Amelia live next door. We both have ocean views. The other suite doesn't, but we make up for it with butler service."

"Pretty swank," she said. But Michaela wasn't prepared for just how swank it was. After Marcus opened the door, she gaped at the entire living room wall. It was a floor to ceiling window overlooking Kaanapali beach with views of Molokai and Lanai.

"I would stand here all day," she said.

"No, you wouldn't. As soon as there was a big surf break, you'd be out there."

She laughed. He was right.

He came up behind her and cupped her shoulders, rubbing his thumbs over them. She nearly crumpled into a puddle.

"Don't be nice to me," she whispered.

"Why?"

"I need to be pissed or I'll start crying."

He moved her pony tail and pressed a kiss to the back of her neck. "I like being nice to you." He caressed her arms and then hugged her from behind. "Now, tell me why you're breathing fire today."

She tensed in his arms. "I was just starting to calm down."

"Let's see if I can help you relax, then." He licked her ear and then nuzzled her neck. He traced circle patterns on her stomach. Michaela's brain short circuited and the anger switched in to lust. She went to turn in his arms, but he held her firm.

"Put your hands on the window," he ordered.

"What?" Michaela asked, breathlessly. He nibbled on the juncture between her shoulder and neck and it was making her crazy.

"Do it." He slid his hands under her bikini top and groaned in her ear.

She smacked her hands on the window just to keep her balance as he massaged her breasts.

"I've been thinking about these all night," he said, rubbing his palms over her hard nipples.

She swayed back against his erection and smiled at how hard he was.

He continued to ravage that sweet spot on her neck while he rolled one of her nipples between his thumb and forefinger.

"Oh," she moaned. Her vision was filled with the deep blue sky and the turquoise waves. Spots of white water dotted over the ocean as the waves crashed against the reefs.

Marcus pressed in closer, reaching down into her bikini bottom.

"Spread your legs," he ordered, and she was powerless to do anything but obey him.

He crooked his fingers between her legs and played with her. Michaela's head arched back, and he kissed her cheek and forehead.

"Come for me," Marcus commanded, his fingers dancing inside her. The tug on her nipple and the flicking against her clit was bringing her fast to a dangerous edge. She backed up against him, rubbing her ass over his hardness.

The only sound in the room was her harsh breathing and the slick sounds he was making in her body.

"Fuck, you're wet," he ground out.

She reached up and held his head next to hers. "I'm coming," she gasped.

"Yeah," Marcus said, not letting up one bit.

Pleasure as bright as the sun, blinded her and her entire body trembled.

"Mmm." Marcus brought his fingers to his mouth and tasted her.

Whirling, Michaela knocked his hand away and kissed him. She unbuttoned his pants, while his mouth made love to her.

A quiet knock brought Marcus's attention away from her. The door opened, and a woman pushed a breakfast cart inside.

"Breakfast," she said. "*Aloha* Mr. Kincaide."

"Fuck," he whispered and buttoned himself back up, while his back was to the woman. "*Aloha*, Pololena."

Michaela stifled a giggle and fixed her bikini as Pololena noisily set the cart up and pulled over two chairs. Marcus winced as he shifted his erection, and smiled at Michaela ruefully.

Pololena poured coffee into two mugs. "Will there be anything else, sir?"

"We're good for now," Marcus said without turning around. "Thank you, Pololena."

After she left, Marcus locked the door.

Michaela raised her eyebrow.

"Should have done that in the first place," he said. He advanced back on her with a determined gleam in his eyes. And his phone rang.

Don't answer it.

He took another step.

Don't fucking answer it.

He took it out of his pocket and looked at it. "I've got to take this."

It's a good thing his window didn't open, because she was seriously considering throwing him out of it. Or at least his phone.

75

"Dig in," he said without looking at her. "I'm going to take this and get changed."

What the hell?

She wondered why he didn't want to continue where they left off, but then her stomach growled, and she quickly got over any insecurity when she saw the pineapple spears.

Marcus came back, looking like he hopped into a quick shower before changing into a battered T-shirt and board shorts. She didn't feel at all guilty that she ate all the pineapple.

He sat down across from her. "Sorry about that."

"What was so important that you couldn't ravish me first and then take the call?" Michaela was only half serious.

"We're renovating the last building, and the contractors need me to hold their dicks."

"There's an image."

He rolled his eyes. "I'd rather walk them through it then have to redo their work because the foreman is fishing today."

"It sounds like a clusterfuck."

"They keep telling me it'll get done island time. Which is the polar opposite from New York time."

"I'm sorry," she said. "If you want to back out of today, I understand. I guess all I needed was a mind blowing orgasm to get over my ex being a prick."

"Not a chance," he said. "I didn't bring you up here to seduce you. But you were so damned gorgeous, I couldn't help myself."

"I'm not complaining," she said and took a bite of her omelet. She closed her eyes in appreciation. "Oh man, that's good."

Michaela opened her eyes to find him staring at her with sheer lust.

"So much for the cold shower."

"We didn't have to stop," she said.

Marcus took in a shuddering breath. "If Pololena hadn't interrupted us, I'd already be inside you."

Oh hell yeah.

She tossed down her fork. "Let's go."

Marcus held up his hand. "I promised to take you surfing. We're going on a date. We should have gone to dinner last night, but I got called away. I want to make it up to you. Eat first. Then surf. Then sex," he said.

"Sounds like a perfect day." Michaela ran her toes up his calf.

He groaned. "You're killing me, you know that?"

She sighed dreamily. "You are great for my ego. Thanks for turning my day around. I had a fight with my ex."

Marcus's jaw clenched and he scanned her face. "He hit you?"

"What?" Michaela looked up from her eggs in shock. "No, of course not. He was being a dick. On the phone. Per usual." She shook her head. "I don't want to talk about him. What's done is done." And if that meant that the local gangs were wearing her trousseau, well she hoped they enjoyed them. Maybe she'd sue Gerald for the cost over it for breach of contract. The thought made her giggle.

"What?"

"Having revenge fantasies about my ex."

"I don't want you thinking about him at all today. Any fantasies you have are just going to be you and me."

"That sounds awesome." Michaela's body was still humming from his touch. It was hot that he was willing to wait to get his pleasure. A lot of guys would have just boned her on the couch. Not that she would've minded that, but it made her feel special that he actually wanted to spend time with her.

"How did it go with you and the guy that was pissing your brother off?

"Tetsuo?" Marcus' lips compressed. "He's a grade-A cocksucker. He's a local businessman with connections that let him get away with damn near everything. He once cut a parasail line on a boat that we were taking out."

"Holy shit." Michaela almost spilled her coffee.

"It could have ended much worse. My sister-in-law, Amelia, was up a couple of hundred feet when it happened. We were able to pull her down safely, but she got dunked into the water. Samuel was able to get her untangled from the sail before she drowned."

"Are you sure it was Tetsuo that did it?"

"He pretty much admitted it."

"Why didn't you turn him in?" she asked.

"He owns the cops. Then he kidnapped Amelia and made us sell the Palekaiko Beach Resort to him."

"That's totally illegal. It would never hold up in court. You signed under duress."

Marcus shrugged. "He owns the courts, too. And I can't deal with the fucking lawyers."

She considered stabbing him with her fork, but she had better uses for it and took the last piece of dragon fruit instead.

"Wait," she said, after finishing the succulent fruit. "I thought you and Dude were the owners of the Palekaiko Beach Resort?"

"We are now. Tetsuo made a deal that if we could make a profit for him, basically double what he paid us for the resort, he would allow us to buy it back."

"So what happened?"

"Amelia is a machine. We met his goals and paid his outrageous selling price. We figured that was the end of it." He dusted his hands. "Good riddance."

"Let me guess. He got to thinking about how he should have asked for more money or that he should have refused to sell it back to you all together."

"Well, he was pretty much honor bound to sell it back to us after the promise he made."

Michaela snorted. "Men like that don't care about promises."

"Maybe not, but they care about their reputation and if it got around that Tetsuo Hojo doesn't keep his promises, his business ventures would suffer."

"What about your business ventures? You guys took a huge hit on this place."

Marcus nodded. "Yeah, my board of directors isn't very happy with me. But he's my brother, so what can you do?"

"Dude must love this place."

Marcus almost choked on his coffee. "He likes sitting on his ass in that hammock, but he wants out. He'd like to sell the resort, buy a condo, and call it a day."

"I don't get it," Michaela said. "Why did you buy the place back from Tetsuo then?"

"Amelia."

"You guys bought a Maui resort for her?" Michaela was stunned.

"It was her dream to run a resort like this. If we hadn't, she probably would have gone to work for Tetsuo, and then she'd have to answer to him. Samuel wasn't going to allow that."

Her heart hurt a little. What would it be liked to be loved like that?

"But that doesn't mean that we can all sit on our asses in a hammock and drink beer all day. We're in the red, and we've poured way too much money into this place. These newest renovations just might tank us if we can't fill them as soon as they're completed."

She reached across the table and put her hand on top of his. "It's beautiful here. You'll have no problem filling them up."

He blew out a breath. "You'd think that, but any more bad luck and we're in real trouble."

"Okay, enough business talk. So tell me about Ho'okipa. What made you choose there for our surfing adventure?"

"I was originally going to try Olowalu today. It's got a nice break, but you said you were looking for some big waves so we're going to the North Shore. Besides, Olowalu is sharky under normal conditions."

Michaela cleared her throat. "I hear it's too crowded there anyway."

He grinned. "You'll like Ho'okipa. It has a strong rip and a shallow reef. We're going to hit the Pavilions. There's some big waves out there today. You think you can handle that?"

"Bring it."

"It will take us about an hour to get there. I figure we could have dinner at Mama's Fish House."

"Do they have malasadas for dessert?"

"Not that I recall, but they tell you the name of the fisherman that catches your dinner."

"I think I'm a little underdressed for dinner."

"So let's go back to your hotel and grab a change of clothes for you too. And maybe an overnight bag."

Shit, now what was she going to do? She couldn't bring him back to the room without getting Amelia in trouble.

"What's the dress code like? I don't have anything fancy."

"Not too fancy," he said. "A sun dress should be fine."

She bit her lip. "My hotel is really far away. I don't want to risk having the wind pick up. We're already late getting started."

Marcus shrugged. "All right. But I want to take you to a nice restaurant. How about tomorrow night?"

That should give her enough time to go shopping. Even if she had to call a cab.

"I'm in." Michaela balled up her napkin and placed it on her plate. "That was delicious."

"You're delicious," he said. "Come on, let's hit the North Shore before I forget I'm a gentleman."

Chapter Seven

MARCUS HAD A HARD ON AGAIN BY the time they pulled into the parking spot. Michaela was so fucking sexy in that little bikini. He parked at the lookout first, so they could watch for a bit.

"Not that I'm complaining," he said as they walked to the edge of the cliff. "But aren't you afraid of losing the suit in the water?"

She grinned up at him, so fucking beautiful with the sun on her face and the wind in her hair. When she stormed through the lobby this morning and asked for Hani, there was no way in hell Marcus was going to let her go out without him today. She was so fired up about her ex, that it was all he could do to keep his hands off her once they had been alone.

"It's made for surfing. My next one isn't going to be white though."

"The white suits you." He liked the contrast between it and his tanned arm.

"White isn't my lucky color," she said sadly.

Marcus stood behind her and wrapped his arms around her. He rested his cheek against hers and was delighted when her breathing quickened when he pressed his body against hers.

"Those waves crashing in are white." He kissed her cheek.

Michaela trailed her fingers over his arms and the tickling went straight to his cock.

"Think it's too windy to surf?" he asked.

"Not on your life," she said, taking him by the hand. "Come on."

He was about to unhook the boards, when she got back into the car. "It's easier to walk from here," he said.

She crooked her finger at him.

Marcus got back in and closed the door. "Second thoughts?"

Reaching over, she slid her hand into his shorts and grabbed him. "Michaela," he gasped like an old lady clutching her pearls. "People can see us."

"No," she said, leaning over so their faces were almost touching. "They can't see that I'm jerking you off. So as long as you don't kiss me or anything, it will look like we're just talking."

She had his cock in a tight grip and was stroking him leisurely.

"Holy shit," he said. He was getting a hand job in his car like a teenager at a drive-in. Not that he was complaining. It felt so good, his eyes were crossing.

"Just look at me and smile."

"Fuck that feels good." He arched into her.

Michaela's chocolate brown eyes danced with glee. "Too bad it's not dark. I'd have my mouth around you right now."

He sucked in a breath and groaned.

"I like how you feel. So nice and hard."

"Michaela," he moaned. She was driving him crazy. He turned to cup her breast in his hand. He rubbed his thumb against her nipple.

"Public indecency," she warned. "Hands off."

He growled, and she punished him by rubbing faster.

"I'm going to fuck you so hard, we're going to break my bed," he vowed.

"Keep talking tough guy."

He tossed his shirt over his head and tugged down on his shorts to give her better access.

"God, you're gorgeous," she said in a reverent tone that made his balls clench. "I want to lick every muscle on your body."

She rubbed her thumb over the tip that was moistened with his pre come. Marcus didn't recognize the noise coming out of his mouth. It was half growl, half moan with an undertone of begging. He had no more words. He was lost in the pleasurable friction she was building in him.

"Your eyes are so intense," Michaela whispered.

He wanted to see her face when she made him come. It wouldn't be long now. He had taken care of himself in the shower because he had been iron hard even after talking to the contractors, but her touch was driving him over the edge, past reason. And that dirty mouth of hers. Marcus gave a low chuckle. He had plans for that.

"You're playing with fire," he warned her.

"Did you think I'd let you have all the fun? Now, it's your turn to come for me."

He didn't care who the fuck saw, he dove in and kissed her as he exploded all over her hand and his chest. Breathing heavily, he dropped back on his seat.

Michaela licked her fingers and his cock twitched at the sight.

"You're going to kill me." Reaching for his shirt, he wiped himself off with it, and tossed it in the back seat. "Don't make me forget that back there. That's all I need is Samuel finding it."

She laughed.

"There should be tissues in the glove box." Marcus tucked himself back into his shorts.

He kissed her again because she tasted like pineapples and her lips were addicting. "You're amazing."

"It's hard not to jump on you," she admitted. "You're so damn sexy."

"What are you doing for breakfast tomorrow?" Marcus wasn't going to let her out of his sight.

"Hopefully you," Michaela said.

"Good answer."

"Let's hit the waves." The most perfect woman in the world said, and then climbed out of his car.

□□□

High on endorphins and adrenaline, Michaela took her first wave. The exhilaration hit as she caught it. Pushing up to a standing position, she got her balance. The roar of the ocean was in her ear and the spray of the water in her face. She was in front of the break and feeling good about the ride. Dropping down the face of the wave, she left her stomach at the peak.

Cowabunga, her heart cried.

She was so glad she was here and not on a cramped flight back home. She steadied herself to turn, so she carved ahead of the white water, but it was too fast for her and a waterfall of ocean curved over her head. Adapting, Michaela rode through the gas chamber, trailing her hand until she shot out the other side and managed a few more turns before the ocean was done with her and pushed her off the board. She fell safely. Marcus had prepared her to expect the violent rush of water sending her tumbling, but she hadn't expected a second wave to keep her down. Resisting the urge to panic, she swam through it even though she wasn't sure which way was up. When her hand broke water, she pushed herself the rest of the way to the surface, taking a huge breath once her head crested. Her surfboard was close, and she slithered on top of it, paddling out of the wave line to catch her breath.

She was exhausted and her arms were shaking, but she was laughing and crying at the same time. It had been too long since she experienced the raw power of Mother Nature. Reining in the hysterics, Michaela sat up on her board to watch Marcus. He was right behind her, but she didn't see him in the water.

Then she saw him burst out of a tube, his board dancing across the top of the waves. He rode it to the end like a man taming a bucking bronco. Finishing it up, he leaned back and pivoted out of the wave like a boss.

Michaela waved to get his attention, and he paddled over to where she was resting.

"Now I know why they call you the *Kahuna*," she leaned over and kissed him.

He held her head when she would have pulled away and continued the kiss.

"Bikini's still on, I see," he said when he was done kissing her senseless.

"You can take it off anytime you want," she purred.

"I plan on it. Let's grab a few more waves first."

There wasn't a lot of time for talking. The waves were coming fast and high. It was everything she could do to keep getting back on her board after turtle rolling through the incoming waves so she didn't get pushed back to the beach. Michaela was out of practice for the hard stuff. Too much sitting behind a desk and in the law library.

"Hey, Kincaide?"

Marcus looked up at a big Hawaiian in the lineup.

"Yeah?"

"Tetsuo sends his regards." He gave him a slow shaka.

Marcus returned the gesture. "Give him my best."

The guy laughed and paddled into position for the peak.

"Was it just me, or did that sound ominous?" Michaela asked.

"Just ignore it. His goons like to make veiled threats disguised as being friendly or helpful. Still, it couldn't hurt to stay away from him."

"Will do."

They still had to wait an hour to get into position again. This time she let Marcus go first so she could see him. The Hawaiian came out of nowhere and dropped in on him.

"Hey," she yelled.

Marcus saw and tried to avoid him, but the guy was fast. He squatted down and pulled Marcus's ankle leash and sent Marcus went flying into the surf. The guy went to ride over him, but Marcus was out of the way, albeit in the soup.

"Did you see that bullshit?" Michaela said, but no one made eye contact.

She took her turn, but her concentration was off because she kept looking over her shoulder to see if some asshole was burning her. However, she had a good ride and was starting to get a feel for the pace. Marcus was waiting for her this time. He was glowering at the Hawaiian who had dunked him.

"Are you all right?" she asked.

"Yeah, I'm fine. That shithead just wants to play head games with me."

"Do you want to go?"

"Fuck no. I'm not letting some kook yank my leash and get away with it."

"Please don't kick your board at him. It's dangerous."

"Not the way I do it," he said. "I don't aim for the body. I aim for the board. They still hit the waves, but no injuries."

"Don't play games. We can go to another spot," she said. Pissing matches never ended well.

"Do you feel safe?"

"Yeah," she said.

"Are you having a good time?"

Michaela nodded. "The best."

"Then we're staying."

He was so stubborn, she wanted to scream.

"You go first," he said. "I want to watch and make sure they don't try anything funny with you. I'll be close enough to burn them if they do."

"Be careful. It's not worth it. I can take a dunking. It wouldn't be the first time." Most of the time, the people she encountered surfing were the nicest and laid back people she'd ever met. Then there were other times, when some misogynistic jerkoff thought he owned the ocean.

"Not on my watch," Marcus said.

But by the time they got back up to the break, the guy was nowhere in the lineup. The tension eased from her chest, and she held hands with Marcus while they studied the waves. There were a bunch of people ahead of them, so it was another long wait for a wave.

"Have I mentioned that I'm going to fuck you against the wall as soon as we get back to my place?" he said in her ear.

"You've been thinking about this all this time?" she asked, rubbing her thumb over his wrist.

"I've been alternating between that and with eating your sweet pussy and having you ride me."

She shivered as his rough voice tingled through her. If she was crazy for sleeping with a man she just met, Michaela didn't care. Even if it turned out to be a one-night stand, it was better sex than doing herself or going back to Gerald.

"How am I supposed to be all Zen like and ride the wave like a surf goddess while I'm thinking of your cock?" she whispered back in his ear.

Eventually it was her turn on the wave again and she was in perfect position. She popped up quickly and saw a stranger snaking in on her.

Shit.

She was going to have to do some tricky maneuvers to avoid him. He was heading right for her.

"Behind you," Marcus yelled.

Whipping around, she saw Marcus on her six. He was coming in low and fast. The three of them were on a collision course.

Marcus maneuvered around her easily, cutting fast and putting himself between her and the stranger who seemed to be gunning for them. For a moment, Michaela thought it was just some Barney being a dick, but as Marcus surfed closer, the man kicked his board at him.

Michaela shrieked and hit the water, not wanting any part of that. The wave pummeled her over, but she was expecting to feel like a rag doll in a washing machine so she relaxed and went with the flow. When she made it out of the white water, she immediately looked around for the Marcus and the stranger.

The stranger was gone, but Marcus was paddling in towards the shore. As she caught up with him, she saw the blood.

Oh no. Sharks would be zeroing in on that soon, if they hadn't already.

Not caring that she looked like a gremmie, she kicked with one leg as she paddled to catch up with him.

"Marcus," she cried.

His scalp was cut open down to his forehead. It had just missed his eye. "Took the fin on the top of my head," he muttered. "It looks worse than it is."

"Let's get you out of here."

"I'm going to need you to drive. I'm shorry," he cleared his throat. "Sh-sh-orry."

"Okay, that's enough. Don't talk." He was slurring his words and his eyes kept rolling back in his head. They hit the shallows, and she started yelling. "I need an ambulance. Help!"

"I'm fine," he said. "I just need to take a nap." He rested his head on his arms.

"No," she cried. "Wake up." Michaela splashed him and tugged him on his board to shore.

She kept looking over her shoulder to see if the blood had attracted any sharks, but she didn't see a fin or a shadow. "Help!" she cried again. "Blood in the water. Head injury. Marcus, please wake up." She shook his arm.

"Leave me alone, Michaela. I need to get shome shleep."

"You have a concussion. You need to stay awake. Help!"

"Shtop yelling. I have a headache."

Finally, the life guards heard her, and they ran with a stretcher to Marcus.

Chapter Eight

AS THEY PUT MARCUS IN THE AMBULANCE, Michaela leaned down and kissed him. "I'll be right behind you."

"Love you," he muttered.

She froze, gaping at him. Two years and Gerald never said those words to her. It's been three days. No one falls in love in three days.

He's delirious.

He thinks you're someone else.

Michaela couldn't think about it right now. But damn, did her heart want to. Tossing Marcus' beach towel over his leather seat, she slid into the driver's side and adjusted the seat and mirror.

As she followed the ambulance to the urgent care facility in Kihei, she fumbled to turn Marcus' phone on. The beeps and buzzes sounded for a good three minutes as his notifications caught up. She took her eyes off the road long enough to scroll through his contents and find Amelia's name. Putting the phone in the cradle mounted on the dashboard, she toggled on the speaker phone.

Thankfully, Amelia answered on the first ring. "I don't have the fucking numbers for you, yet."

"Amelia, it's Michaela."

"Michaela? Why are you on Marcus' phone?"

"There's been an accident. No, that's not true. One of Tetsuo's goons shot his surfboard at Marcus' head."

"What? Marcus has been shot in the head?"

"No. He's got a concussion, and his head is split open from being hit by a surfboard."

"Does he need stitches?"

"I think so. It was bleeding so much. We're going to the urgent care center now. He's in an ambulance. I'm driving his car."

"We'll be there as soon as we can."

"Wait," Michaela cried. "Don't hang up. Can you bring him a change of clothes? He's going to be freezing. He doesn't have anything with him but his bathing suit."

"Not a problem."

"And, I hate to ask this, but could you bring me a cover up or a dress, too? I'm in a bikini and a towel."

"You got it. I'm going to fax or email Marcus' medical information to them and then we'll be on our way."

"Okay," Michaela said.

"Are you sure Tetsuo is behind this?" Amelia asked.

"Pretty sure."

"Stay safe. We'll be there as soon as we can."

□□□

"I can't believe they stapled my head," Marcus groaned.

"I offered to do it," Samuel said, "But for some reason they turned me down."

Marcus' head was throbbing, even with the extra strength Tylenol and the lidocaine numbing his head. "You brought me pants. You've helped enough." He was pretty sure Amelia had

93

picked out the clothes. Samuel would have brought neon green and pink plaid Bermuda shorts, if left to his own devices.

Marcus had still been pretty out of it when Amelia and Samuel burst in. Amelia had immediately taken Michaela away, which he would have protested if he hadn't been so damned loopy. His head was a little clearer now. All he wanted to do was go home and sleep for a week, preferably with Michaela snuggled up next to him.

Fucking cock blocked by Tetsuo Hojo.

"When can I get out of here?"

"They're discharging you now. You get to be woken up every couple of hours for the next day. Plus, no strenuous activities. That means, no surfing or playing tonsil hockey with the *wahine* in the teeny bikini."

"Where is Michaela?"

"I had Amelia drive her back to her hotel."

"What? Why?" Marcus tried to stand but the floor rushed up to meet his head.

Samuel caught him before he could face plant and muscled him back into his chair. "That's why."

"Tetsuo knows who she is. She's not safe. What if he kidnaps her?"

"Calm down. For all we know, it was just some aggro in the lineup that had nothing to do with Tetsuo. Michaela said the guy who hit you wasn't the same one that pulled your leash."

"Do you believe that?" Marcus felt nauseous as hell and wished the room would stop spinning.

"No. I think the fucking coward was behind this. But Michaela is too new for him to try and ransom her back to us."

94

"Pay it," he snarled. "Promise me. If I'm out of it, you'll pay whatever he wants to keep her safe."

Samuel held up his hands. "Easy. I'll see what I can do."

"I don't have her number," Marcus said. "I don't know where she's staying. Or how long she'll be in Maui. Or where she's from. I don't know anything about her."

"It's okay. I'm sure Amelia will get the skinny on her. You know how she is."

"What if she doesn't?" Marcus stood up, managing not to sway this time. He hated feeling weak. "I'm afraid Michaela's spooked, and I'll never see her again. Text Amelia and tell her to get her information. Have her send her a dozen roses too."

Samuel blinked at him. "Are you feeling all right?"

"No, you ass. My head almost got knocked off by a surfboard. The subcontractors are dicking around on the renovations, and my girl doesn't know she's mine yet."

"Yup," Samuel said. "I can see where that would be a problem. How long has she been your girl, since you don't know a damned thing about her?"

Marcus frowned. His knees wobbled and he sat back down. "My head hurts."

The nurse came in at that moment with a wheelchair. "Here are your exit papers. Please follow all instructions and pay close attention to what the pain prescription says."

Marcus' locked gazes with his brother. "What type of painkillers?"

"After the first twenty-four hours, he can take OxyContin. Before that, though, no more than eight hundred milligrams of Tylenol."

Marcus heard the roar of the ocean between his ears. Samuel shot to his feet and stood chest to chest with the nurse.

"No," Samuel said. "Rip up the prescription. He doesn't want it."

"You are not his doctor."

"No, I'm his brother. He used to be addicted to opiate pain killers."

Marcus flinched. That made him sound like a douchebag. It was more complicated than that. Actually, it had been pretty easy. It started out harmless, until it wasn't.

"He can't have them. Tylenol will be fine."

The nurse opened and closed his mouth. "That should be on his chart and in his medical records."

"It's not something we like to have written down," Samuel said.

Yeah, God forbid there was something written down that might embarrass his father's political career.

"You better rethink that. In a different circumstance, he could have been given them without anyone knowing the harm we were causing."

"It was a long time ago," Marcus said, hating how his head was swimming. He didn't need Samuel to fight his battles. "Over ten years." He had been in high school, playing football. Tore his ACL to shit. And being young and stupid, he went back to playing too soon. When the prescriptions ran out, there were always other doctors willing to give a rich kid a break.

He took a deep breath. It was another lifetime. Another Marcus. It was so tempting. It had been a long time. He could handle two. Just to take the edge off the pain.

"All it takes is one pill," Samuel said.

"You don't know that," Marcus argued.

"I know you're not getting them, so shut the fuck up."

Marcus held up his hands in surrender. "Can I go now?"

Chapter Nine

MICHAELA CONNED AMELIA INTO TAKING HER TO WALMART. She bought a cheap suitcase and enough clothes to last her a week and a half. She wouldn't be winning any fashion awards, but she'd be comfortable.

"Don't suppose a real room opened up yet?" she asked as they got into the car again.

"Sunday," Amelia promised.

"It doesn't have to be a suite," she said.

"I'm going to take care of you. It means a lot to me that you were there with Marcus. Is there something going on between the two of you?" Amelia gave the shaka to a driver who let her pull out into the street ahead of him.

Love you.

Marcus said that. It made Michaela all giggly, to think about that. Even if she was pretty sure it was because Marcus just had his bell rung, and was probably picturing spreadsheets when he said it.

"It's too soon to tell." But his words made her rethink everything. She had been willing to settle for Gerald, more for her father's sake than anything else. Gerald never wanted to be naughty in the car or take her surfing. He certainly wouldn't have gotten her off without wanting immediate reciprocation. She didn't love Marcus, but she loved the all burning sexual frenzy that came over her when he touched her. He had said he wanted an intense affair. She was on board with that. Perhaps, it might lead to something more. But for the moment, she was content to enjoy his attention.

"I'm sorry I'm making you lie to him."

"He really hasn't asked much about me," Michaela realized. How could he love her? He didn't even know where she lived or what she did for a living. It was silly to get all gushy about words a concussed man mumbled. "I've been able to side step his questions, and he doesn't push."

"I'm just afraid if we tell him, he'll kick you out."

"I don't think he'll do that, but he might feel obligated to have me shack up with him, and I'm not ready for that type of pressure." Although, it could have gotten to that level pretty damned quick. Or it would have, before Marcus' head wounds.

Samuel called while Amelia was driving. She let it go to voice mail and then found a spot to pull over and listen to it. The boys were on their way back from the hospital. Marcus was groggy and in pain, but he'd have a bunch of people looking in on him tonight. She'd offered to help and Amelia gave her the morning shift. Michaela was grateful because she was bone tired.

They stopped at Zippy's on the way back from Walmart. Michaela was a little disappointed that was about as exotic as a Denny's, but the food was good. And the malasadas at the end of the meal made up for it. Both of them took home a bag stuffed full of the little doughnuts.

After they got back to the resort, Amelia hurried to make everything ready for Marcus' arrival. Michaela hauled her suitcase up the stairs, pushed through the large plastic sheeting, and let herself into her room. Setting her new stuff on the armchair, she opened the drawer where she had tossed her phone this morning. Had it only been this morning? It seemed like a week.

Michaela stuffed a malasada into her mouth while she checked messages. Three from Gerald.

Lying down on the bed, she stared up at the ceiling and pressed play.

THIS ISN'T LIKE YOU. I'M WORRIED. YOUR FAMILY IS WORRIED. IF YOU'RE NOT COMING HOME, I'M COMING OUT THERE TO FIND YOU.

"Good luck with that," she said with her mouth full.

The next message was equally entertaining.

SANDY SPENT ALL DAY AT YOUR CONDO. YOUR LUGGAGE WAS FINALLY DELIVERED AT FIVE THIRTY. IT'S SAFE IN YOUR BEDROOM. ARE YOU SURE YOU DON'T WANT ME TO BRING IT WHEN I COME DOWN ON SUNDAY? I BOOKED MY FLIGHT, I'LL BE LANDING AT 10:04 A.M. CAN YOU PICK ME UP FROM THE AIRPORT? GIVE ME A CALL. I'VE GOT SOMETHING I WANT TO BOUNCE OFF YOU.

"Bounce this," she said, lifting her left boob in protest. Gerald was going to be in for a fucking surprise on Sunday. A part of her considered picking him up at the airport, if he brought her Victoria Secret lingerie so she could show them off to Marcus. But then the thought of letting him wait without a word from her seemed like poetic justice.

Michaela pressed play on the last message, wondering what else he had to say.

HEY, STILL WAITING FOR YOUR CALL. SANDRA WASN'T ABLE TO FIND YOUR ENGAGEMENT RING.

"You had her rifle through my things?" she shouted. Then had to replay the message because she missed what he said next.

I HOPE YOU'RE STILL WEARING IT. I THINK WE SHOULD GET MARRIED ON THE BEACH OUT THERE.

"Not a chance."

BUT IN ANY EVENT, I JUST WANTED TO KNOW IT WAS SAFE. THAT RING COST ME TEN GRAND. NOT THAT YOU'RE NOT WORTH IT. JUST GIVE ME A CALL AND LET ME KNOW YOU STILL HAVE IT.

"I still have it. It's in a crushed box on my floor."

Except it wasn't.

Michaela flew off the bed and searched for it. It wasn't there. It wasn't under the bed or in any of the drawers. Her trash can was empty also.

She called Joely's number.

"Hey Michaela, I heard you dented the *Kahuna's* head."

"Not me, one of Tetsuo's goons did."

"Shut the front door," she said.

"No lie. The reason I'm calling, though, is did you happen to see a ring box on my floor when you cleaned up in here today?"

"I was off today. Let me check with Kevan. Why? Is it missing?"

"Yeah. It had my engagement ring in it."

"Shit!" Joely said. "I'll try and track him down. He's a fuckwit. If it was on the floor, there's a good chance he tossed it. The good news is the dumpsters don't empty until tomorrow morning. The bad news is we're at capacity. I'll round up the troops and see if we can help. Meantime, check the dumpster out by your building. He might have gotten lazy and tossed it into the contractor's dumpster."

"Okay, thanks." Michaela stuffed her phone back into her pocket. "Ten thousand reasons why I should give a fuck about this ring," she muttered, as panic fluttered through her. She ran down the stairs, and went over to the dumpster.

Opening it up, Michaela gagged from the stench. There were boards and wires in there, but Joely had pegged it. There were also three large garbage bags in there that looked like they could be from the hotel rooms. Of course, Michaela couldn't reach them. Looking around, she found some old pails from Home Depot she could stack and then stand on. Wobbling on them, she steadied herself on the side of the dumpster, throwing her leg over before hopping inside.

Holding her breath, she tore the first bag apart. Gross. She wished she had gloves on. Hell, a full hazmat suit would have worked for her too. The malasadas threatened to make a reappearance, but she kept it together. There was rotted fruit and empty boxes and cups. It looked like it was beach garbage.

Great.

She was poking through the second bag when she felt that someone was watching her. Looking up, she saw a man in a security uniform coming towards her.

Fu-uck.

There was no way she was going to hop out of here and make a run for it, so she continued looking through the trash. She was on the third bag, when she caught sight of something that could be the ring box.

"Ma'am, you're not allowed to be in there," the guard said. His name badge said Holt. Crap, this was the guy she had to avoid so he didn't tattle to Marcus.

"I know. I'm sorry. I accidentally threw something important away and I'm trying to find it."

He shone a flashlight in there. "Are you a guest?" he asked her.

"No, I was on the beach today and I think I threw out my ring by mistake."

"Your ring?"

"I think it's here." She poked through the bag, desperate to find the stupid ring box.

"Please step out of the dumpster," he said in a polite voice that brooked no bullshit. He was nice enough to hold out his hand to help her out and he didn't even gag at what was all over her Walmart sneakers. "You're going to want to stay out of the garbage. Once the sun goes down the rats come out."

"What?" Michaela jumped back on the home depot buckets and nearly took a header. Holt steadied her on her feet.

Her phone rang. She looked up at him, apologetically. Taking it out of her pocket, Michaela saw it was Joely. "I should get this." She answered it. "Hi, I can't talk right now."

"I've got your ring. Kevan put it in the resort's safe in Amelia's office."

"Great. That's a big relief." She pulled the phone away from her mouth to talk to Holt. "My friend found my ring."

"Ma'am, I'm afraid I'm going to have to escort you off the property," Holt said, holding out his hand.

"Who's that?" Joely asked.

"Oh, that won't be necessary, Holt," Michaela said. "I can make my way out."

"Oh shit," Joely groaned.

No kidding.

"I insist" There was a little more steel in Holt's voice this time.

"I'll call you back," Michaela said, disconnecting the call.

She ignored his hand and started walking, wondering if she should wade in the water with her sneakers on to clean them off, but the shark signs were still up.

"They didn't open the beach today?" Michaela asked Holt, since he was tagging along behind her like a baby duck. A big, burly, baby duck.

"Nope."

"Isn't that a little odd?"

"Yep."

Well, he was a great conversationalist. At the edge of the property, he stopped and said, "Have a nice night, Ma'am."

Michaela waved. "You too."

Chapter Ten

MARCUS HAD A REALLY SHITTY NIGHT. Every two fucking hours, he had to tell someone that he hadn't slipped into a coma. He wanted to wrap his hands around Tetsuo's neck. He wanted to sleep for days. He wanted Michaela. He wanted those fucking white pills.

No, he didn't.

He just wanted the pain to go away.

But that wasn't true either.

He just wanted the Oxy.

He crunched two more Tylenols, hoping the bitter taste would turn his stomach to the thought of the pills. But all they did was make him want to chase the taste away with Scotch. To make matters worse, he was getting the runaround again from his useless as tits on a bull lawyer. He'd half a mind to fire the asshole, but then they would have to start again from scratch. All he needed was some leverage to make Tetsuo back off until they could finish the final renovations and start to market heavily to bring in the tourists.

Holt let himself in. "Are you supposed to be on the computer?"

"I figured if I was going to be up, I might as well be productive. Were you able to find out any information on Michaela?"

Launching himself on the couch, Holt put his feet up on the coffee table. "You got a problem."

"You mean aside from the six staples in my head?"

"I found her."

Marcus swiveled in his chair. "Is she staying at the Hilton?" That would be why she was close by.

Holt shook his head. "I stumbled across her last night while I was doing rounds. She was dumpster diving on our property."

"What?" Marcus said. "That doesn't make any sense." Even though it hurt, he racked his brain to figure out what she actually said to him. "She's on vacation." Actually, she never said that. All he knew was she had a pain in the ass ex and she wanted to get away from the rat race. "What was she doing in the dumpster?"

If he said looking for food, he'd go nuts. They hadn't had time for lunch or dinner because of Tetsuo.

"She said she was on the beach yesterday and accidentally threw out her ring."

"She wasn't on the beach yesterday. She was with me. Why would she lie?"

Holt ticked off on his fingers. "She borrows boards. She borrowed Joely's wetsuit. She wears really cheap clothing."

Marcus shook his head and then regretted it. Was that why she kept wearing the white bikini? She only had the one?

"She's a transient," Holt finished.

"I won't allow that. I'm going to offer her a job. If Dude can do snorkel lessons, she can be our surf instructor. Clear it with Amelia. I can't deal with her perkiness this morning."

"Marcus, you have to realize she might be conning you. She could be a prostitute. You need to protect yourself. If she was sent by Tetsuo to start another cathouse on the property, we're going to get shut down."

"You're wrong," he said. "She's not a transient. She's a surfer. Check the semi-pro leagues. Her name is Michaela Harris. Find out what hotel she's staying at. It's got to be on the strip."

A thought tugged in the back of his head. She had said her hotel was too far to go to get changed, though.

"I don't know. Check all of them if you can. Google her."

Holt pushed himself to his feet. "I'll run her down. But I'm not going to find her."

"Just do it."

After Holt left, Marcus tried to concentrate on work, but it was no use. He couldn't get Holt's words out of his head. What if she was sent by Tetsuo? The timing fit. She'd be a perfect spy, especially if she was screwing him for information. Slamming the top of his laptop down, Marcus went back to bed. The pounding in his head shouldn't be this bad. Part of him worried that it wasn't pain at all, but a phantom of his addiction rising up after all these years.

As he lay with his eyes closed, he tried to ignore the gnawing voice in his head telling him that relief was only a phone call away. He was pretty sure he could get another prescription.

Scowling, Marcus put the thought out of his mind. It wasn't worth it. Not for this. It wasn't agony. It was just annoyance. He wouldn't have even been thinking of it, if the nurse hadn't brought it up. Now it was like, "Don't think about elephant's knees."

All he needed was to sleep. He was dimly aware of Pololena coming in and taking away his half eaten breakfast. He didn't have much of an appetite because he was exhausted. It hadn't helped that it had been like Grand Central Station in here.

Say what you want about New Yorkers being rude, no one had ever cracked his head open with a surfboard at the Met.

He must have dropped off into sleep because when someone sat on his bed, he jolted awake. An agony of colors exploded in his head.

"Easy," Michaela's sultry voice said.

Was he dreaming? Marcus pried his eyes open. She was wearing a University of Hawaii shirt. It was a garish pink. Her shorts were grey and baggy, but she still looked beautiful.

"I need your number," he croaked.

"Most guys ask me for my sign. Scorpio by the way."

He grabbed his phone off the nightstand. "What is it?"

She rattled off the digits. He programmed them in and hit call. Her pocket rang. "Didn't believe me?" she asked without looking at it.

"Sorry, I realized last night that I didn't have any way of contacting you." He eased up into a sitting position. "I'm a little grumpy this morning."

Michaela squinted at his forehead. "You look like Frankenstein. How does it feel?"

He gave a half shrug. "It's fine." It would be too. It was just the first injury he had like this in a long time. It was no big deal. He just hadn't been expecting the aggro at Ho'okipa. He had gotten cocky. It could have gone a lot worse. She could have been hurt.

"I brought your meds," she said, tossing him a bag of pills. "Want me to get you a glass of water?"

Marcus stopped breathing for a moment. He ripped open the bag and clenched his fist around a bottle of twenty OxyContin pills.

No.

Was Holt right after all? He searched Michaela's face. "Who sent you?"

"Amelia." She walked over to the carafe that Pololena left. "Or you can wash them down with coffee."

Just one.

It couldn't hurt.

The pain would be gone and he'd feel like his old self again. Except his old self was a selfish little shit who hurt his family because he was weak. Marcus wanted to crush the bottle in his hand, but he was afraid if the pills spilled out, he wouldn't be strong enough not to take one.

"Amelia gave you these to give to me?" Marcus couldn't remember if Samuel told Amelia about his prior addiction or not. His parents had been so embarrassed by him, they shipped him off to a rehab center and wouldn't talk to him until he was clean. Samuel had called as often as he could sneak it. He forced himself to stare at the bottle. One pill wouldn't be enough. He'd have to take two or three. He wasn't in that much pain. The Tylenol worked enough that he got a little bit of sleep. All he needed was a little bit more, and that cup of coffee—even though his stomach protested at the thought.

She poured him a cup of coffee and set it on the night table next to him. "No. She's put up a schedule. Every two hours, someone grabs your key and comes up to check on you. I asked her if I could come see you this morning." Michaela held his hand between hers. "I was so worried."

"Where did you get the pills?" he asked. She hadn't reacted with any guilt or belligerence. She was looking at him with her warm, brown eyes, and he didn't see any deceit in them. Just concern. Under other circumstances, he might have gone for a kiss. His gaze dropped to her lips. He still might.

"They were hanging off the peg with your key on it."

"Take these." He handed her the pill bottle. He swallowed the coffee in one long drink. Marcus was feeling strong enough to resist the pull, now. But later he might be tempted, or worse old habits might come back and he'd grab two without even thinking about it.

"You sure?" she asked.

"No, and that's the problem." Marcus called Samuel.

"Jesus Christ, what? It's the crack of ten," Samuel answered after the fifth ring. "Don't you have nursemaids you can call to wipe your ass? I'm hung over."

"Tetsuo sent me a gift." He hung up on his brother because he knew it would piss him off.

The door to his suite slammed open. Michaela jumped in surprise. Samuel came storming in, wearing his boxer shorts. They had palm trees on them.

"You could have gotten dressed," Marcus said.

"What's going on?" Michaela asked.

Samuel's eyes narrowed in on the pills she was holding. "What the fuck?" He ripped them out of her hand.

"Careful," Marcus snarled, sending a bolt of pain through his head.

"Did you take any?" Samuel asked, shaking the bottle.

"No."

"Did you?"

"He said no. Back off." Michaela rounded on him.

"Don't tell me to back off, *wahine*." Samuel pointed at her. "You have no idea what's going on."

"I know some local businessman," she used air quotes around the last two words. "Is trying to get his hands on this property and isn't afraid to get dirty in the process."

"Are you working for Tetsuo?"

"Me?" Michaela said. "No. I haven't had the pleasure of meeting the slimy bastard. Why do you think I'm working for him?"

"Samuel shut up. You're out of line." Marcus was terrified he'd tell Michaela about his past addiction, that she would think he was a spoiled rich boy. Maybe he had been, but he made sure he was the polar opposite now. Business before pleasure, always.

"I think you should leave," Samuel said.

Michaela looked at Marcus. "Do you want me to go?"

Marcus was too damned tired to deal with any of this. "Thanks for checking on me. I'm really out of it and all I want to do is sleep. Ignore Samuel, he's a real prick when he's hungover."

"Okay." She leaned in and kissed him on the cheek. "Feel better."

He felt better enough to pull her down for a real kiss. One that could have gone on a lot longer, but he reluctantly released her because he didn't want to put on a show for his brother.

Samuel walked her out and locked the door. "She's on his payroll."

"Have you been talking to Holt?" Marcus sighed.

"No, I try to avoid him. He's a bigger prick than you are."

"Pour me another cup of Joe." He held out his coffee cup.

"What's the magic word?" Samuel said.

"Do it or I'll kick your ass?"

"That's more than one word. Besides, I think I can take you now."

"Do it, or I'll have Holt kick your ass."

Samuel refilled the coffee and handed it back to him before pouring one of his own. "Jesus, my head is pounding. Maybe I should take one of these." Samuel shook the pill bottle.

"Don't be a fuckstick," Marcus said. "It's not funny."

"How's your head this morning?"

"Hurts."

"Pussy," Samuel called over his shoulder as he went into the bathroom.

"Michaela's not working for Tetsuo," Marcus said after Samuel had flushed the pills down the toilet. It was for the best. Another good night of sleep and he wouldn't even feel the urge. He hoped.

"She's a spy. He hired her to get close to you and slip you these pills."

"She said they were at the desk when she grabbed the key." Marcus took his time finishing his coffee, rather than gulping it down like a madman. He was starting to feel better, even though his head felt like it was going to pound off his shoulders.

"I'll look into it."

"You're going to do work? Did you hit your head too?"

"I'll have Amelia look into it. Same thing." Samuel waved his hand.

"Tetsuo is playing dirty. How did he find out about the pills?"

"He's got ears everywhere. But he's gone too far. I'm sick of his shit," Samuel said. "Let's sell him back the place and let him choke on it. The property taxes are killing us."

112

"Convince Amelia of that and we'll talk." Marcus held out his coffee cup for Samuel to refill.

"I'm getting bored with this island anyway. We can find a property anywhere and Amelia can manage it. I hear Tahiti is nice."

"She loves it here," Marcus said. "And you know as well as I do, no matter where we go there will always be a Tetsuo Hojo."

"He tried to kill you."

"No, he harassed me. If he wanted to kill me, they would have held me under the water until I drowned. Same thing with the pills. If I'm stoned on opiates again, I'm not a threat. He's scared of us, Samuel. He wouldn't be pulling this shit if he wasn't."

Samuel paced, spilling coffee on his rug. "He's trying to get our licenses revoked. First it was the prostitution ring that he was running with our housekeeping staff, then it was the code issues on the renovations."

"And we're still here." Marcus took the filled cup back and after finishing it, felt human again.

"I don't trust the *wahine*. She's got you wrapped up in knots. You barely know her."

"I'm working on that. I'll handle Michaela. In fact, I want to hire her on as a surf instructor. She can stay in employee housing where we can keep an eye on her."

"When she's not on your dick."

"Respect. Or I'll knock *your* head off with a surfboard."

"I'm just saying, you're playing right into Tetsuo's hands if you put her on staff."

"Maybe, maybe not. It's the devil you know. If she is Tetsuo's spy, we'll feed her wrong information. It should be apparent very quickly.

Chapter Eleven

MICHAELA WALKED UP TO AMELIA, WHO was behind the concierge desk. "Is there any way I can rent a car and get it delivered here?"

"What do you need a car for?" Amelia said.

"I'm going after Tetsuo."

"You can't," Amelia said. "He's well guarded and I have no idea where he is."

"Not like that," Michaela grinned. "I'm going to hit him where it hurts." She waggled her fingers. "Lawyer, remember. I'm going to check out the court house and law library in Wailuka and see what I can dig up. Maybe hit the county buildings to look up some records. If there's dirt on him, I'll find it. And there's got to be a reason he wants this property so badly, I'll find out that too."

Amelia tossed her a set of keys. "Take my car. If anyone asks, I sent you out for coffee."

"I'll probably be out all day."

"Good coffee is hard to find. Are you sure you want to do this? It might be dangerous. Do you want to take Makoa or one of the boys with you?"

"No. It's going to be long, boring work."

"Why are you so looking so happy about that? You're supposed to be on vacation."

"I love research and I love gathering information. I just wish I had my laptop."

Amelia unplugged her laptop and wound up the cord. "Here, take mine." She stuffed them into a Palekaiko Beach Resort tote bag.

"Are you sure?"

"Let's get this bastard. Is there anything else I can do for you?"

"If Gerald Stone calls looking for me, you haven't seen me since Sunday when you told me my reservation had been cancelled. Oh, and his ring is in your safe."

"Got it," Amelia said.

□□□

Michaela stretched and rolled the kinks out of her neck. Her eyes stung from staring at the computer screen for the last five hours. Stifling a yawn, she decided to call it quits for the day. Her nose itched from the dust and mold from some of the old records. She had a lot of things to process about Tetsuo Hojo's business, but she didn't want to miss the sunset.

The wind was a refreshing blast against her face, even as it blew her hair into her eyes and mouth. There were two thuggish looking men sitting on the hood of Amelia's car. She pretended that she hadn't been heading over there and casually looked around the parking lot.

Crap on toast. There was no one around. She turned to hurry back into the building, but another thug came out of the door she was about to go into. She had an instant to hope that maybe they were looking for Amelia and not her, but the thug made eye contact and she knew it was on. She recognized it as the man who had given Marcus Tetsuo's regards while they were in Ho'okipa.

"I'm probably going to head out to the beach tomorrow for some surfing, if you'd like to shoot a board at my head." She surreptitiously reached into her bag for her phone.

116

"Mr. Hojo would like to speak with you."

Holding eye contact, Michaela pressed a few buttons, hoping it would redial Marcus. "Is he one of the two gentlemen over there?" She jerked her thumb to the two guys by the car.

And when he looked over, she pulled out the phone. Staring at the screen, she had redialed Gerald. "Fuck," she said, before she could stop herself.

A large hand closed over her phone. "I'm afraid I'm going to have to confiscate this for the time being."

"And why is that?" she asked, with her hands on her hips. Michaela looked around desperately for anyone who could help, but the parking lot was bare and no one was close enough to come to her aid.

"Please come with us."

"How about I just follow you in my car? That way you don't have to drive all the way back here."

The man considered her question. "One of my guys will drive your car. You ride with us."

"I just want to be clear," she said, hoping that he hadn't disconnected the phone call. If Gerald was listening in, maybe he could call the police. "I don't have a choice whether or not to go with you, do I? You're forcing me against my will to meet Tetsuo Hojo?"

"We can do it the easy way. Or the hard way. I prefer the easy way." He pointed to his friends. "They prefer the hard way."

Michaela half expected them to be leering and cracking their knuckles, but they were just waiting for her to decide.

"Where are you taking me?" She gave up, handing him Amelia's keys.

He tossed them to one of the goons and opened the door to a big sedan for her. "Wailea. Mr. Hojo has a property there that he'd like you to see."

Well, she was certainly getting a tour of the island. North Shore yesterday, West Maui today. Hopefully, she wouldn't end up at the emergency room again.

"Can I have my phone back?" she asked.

"After your meeting with Mr. Hojo."

She had a feeling if she whipped out the laptop to try and send an email, it would go flying out the window. So she spent the next half hour trying not to let her imagination get away with her. Was this how they kidnapped Amelia? Would they try and ransom her back to get the Kincaides to sell? What would they do to her when they refused?

She was surprised when they turned into the most luxurious hotel she had ever seen. It was the Kaimana Beach Resort, which ironically was Gerald's first choice as their honeymoon hotel.

"Follow me, please," her kidnapper said, getting out of the car. The valet gave them tickets for both vehicles while Michaela gaped at her surroundings.

The lobby was teak wood with a plush carpet and shining marble on the walkways. Thick couches and pouf ottomans the same color as beach sand were sprinkled around the area. The ocean breeze swayed the palm trees and she could see the blue of the ocean, so bright it almost hurt to look at it.

"How's the surfing here?" she said, craning her neck to get a better look.

"Snorkeling is better, but every now and then you can catch a wave."

The ocean called to her after spending most of the day inside, but she didn't think her host would appreciate her paddling out. They led her into one of the hotel towers and then they took an elevator up to the top floor. Unlike Marcus' suite, there were ten rooms on either side of the hallway. They went to room 1010 and walked in.

Gerald would love this place.

It was oozing with luxury and modern comforts. Not that she didn't like those things, but it was a little cold and impersonal. It looked like every other luxury hotel she had ever been in. She was sure the sheets on the bed were pure Egyptian cotton with a thread count that was closer to flannel than not. The comforter on the bed looked like it was softer than a cloud. There was a state-of-the-art entertainment center and quality artwork on the wall. The lighting was recessed and there was a docking station for a laptop and places to charge electronics. A designer bottle of water was settled into fresh ice on the desk along with a basket of snacks. Fresh flowers bloomed on the night stand, scenting the air with a soft, tropical fragrance.

For someone who had been sleeping on a lumpy mattress with no amenities, she could admire it and look at the bed longingly. But, it didn't have the shabby charm of the Palekaiko Beach Resort. It did have gangsters, though. And they were waiting for her out on the balcony.

A small table was set up and a waitress uncovered the food as they came out. A slim Asian man with a cruel smile and mocking eyes, gestured her to sit across from him. In front of her was a Caesar salad and a glass of sparkling wine.

In theory, she should have thrown it in his face. But she only had a PowerBar and a bag of stale Cheetos since breakfast, so she helped herself to a breadstick and sat down.

"I'm so glad you were able to join me for dinner," he said.

"After reviewing my choices, it seemed the prudent thing to do."

He dismissed the thugs who had brought her here with a wave of his hand. "They can be a little over enthusiastic about my wishes."

"Like shooting a surfboard at someone's head?" Michaela raised an eyebrow at him and dug into her salad.

Tetsuo made a concerned face that was about as fake as her politeness. "I had heard about Mr. Kincaide's accident. How is he doing?"

"He's fine. A little tired, but nothing seems to stop Marcus." The Caesar dressing was easily the best she had ever tasted. The view off the balcony was mesmerizing. She could see the entire beach front and all of the ocean.

"That's Mokapu Beach," he said.

Michaela glanced down at the strip of white. It was no Kaanapali, but it was still beautiful.

"This is a gorgeous resort," she said, sipping her wine. It was a crisp Prosecco and her toes curled in happiness. "World class." If only Marcus had been sitting across from her, instead of the man who brought her here under nefarious purposes, it would have been perfect.

The door to the hotel room opened, and a woman stepped in carrying an ugly suitcase and a familiar carry-on.

"What's going on?" she asked, as the woman placed Michaela's luggage on that big, beautiful bed.

"I heard of your unfortunate situation. I was in the position to help. I'd like to offer you this room free for your length of stay, as a token of my good will."

"Why?" Michaela said. "How do you know I don't already have a room?"

"I have ears everywhere. Especially at the courthouse and records department. Did you find anything interesting today?" He looked at her over his wine glass.

"You seem to be a few years behind in paying your taxes," she said. It was public record.

He shrugged. "I'll get around to paying them before it becomes a problem."

Meaning he was probably greasing palms to keep from receiving dunning notices. What she didn't tell him was she traced back a few holding companies to him and found that he was in a little more financial trouble than his surroundings indicated.

"How did you get my things?" Michaela gestured to the maid who was unpacking her clothes and placing them into drawers. "Or do you have hands everywhere as well?"

"Something like that," he said. "Why are you so interested in my properties?

"Why are you so interested in the Palekaiko Beach Resort?" she countered, pushing aside her salad plate.

Immediately, it was whisked away and a battered lemon chicken dish with rice pilaf was placed in front of her. Michaela tried to show a little restraint, but she was still hungry, so she dug in.

"It used to be mine, you know?"

Michaela nodded and swallowed. "Why did you sell it back to the Kincaides?"

Tetsuo made a face and glared out into the ocean. "I had a moment of weakness, wanting to please my nephews. But even before then, the Palekaiko Beach Resort had been in my family for generations.

Michaela frowned. "According to the land records, before the Kincaides bought it the first time, it was owned by Mel Kawena."

"You have a good memory, Ms. Harris. I'm sure that helps you in your chosen profession. Were you planning on taking the bar exam here?"

She wondered if he really knew she was an attorney, or if he was just fishing. Gerald had been required to get his license to practice in Hawaii from his firm. Her firm was more concerned with California law. They wanted her to specialize in divorce. Michaela was considering it, even though it wasn't really her passion. Corporate law was more to her interest.

She shook her head. "I'm just here on vacation."

"Honeymoon, don't you mean."

Michaela's face froze. "I said what I meant." He must have spies everywhere, as well. She tried to rack her brains to remember who was in the lobby when she told her sob story to Hani.

"Don't be alarmed. It's a small island. We like to talk."

She wondered if Marcus knew. She would have liked to have told him herself.

"What would they tell me about Mel Kawena selling prime real estate to a mainlander?"

Tetsuo's lips twisted in a semblance of a smile. Happy that she scored a direct hit, Michaela went back to devouring the succulent chicken.

"They would tell you a very tiresome story about a family feud. Kawena was my sister's husband. He was a *paniolo*, a cowboy. He seduced my sister away from her family. It was a terrible mistake. Before we knew it, she was pregnant and wanted to marry the fool. My parents gave her the property that is now the Palekaiko Beach Resort. They lived there and raised two boys, Holt and Mike."

Michaela glanced up in surprise. Was it just coincidence? How many other Holts were there on the island?

"So what happened?" she asked, soaking her rice in the yummy lemon sauce before spooning it into her mouth.

"He was a cowboy, not a manager. He drove the resort into the ground and drank away the profits. I got my sister out of that situation, protected the boys and all I got for my trouble was his undying hate."

"You took his family away."

Tetsuo banged his fist on the table.

"He didn't deserve them."

Michaela flinched at the violence in his eyes. She was no longer hungry.

"He sold the resort to the Kincaides to spite me. I would have bailed him out. I would have given them a nice stipend to live on, controlled by myself naturally."

"Naturally," Michaela said.

"It took a while and some planning, but the Kincaides eventually sold the resort to me."

"After you kidnapped Amelia," she said.

123

He gave a half smile, but didn't deny the allegations.

"If you think Marcus is going to sell it to you because you kidnapped me..."

Tetsuo laughed in her face.

Swallowing her anger, she glared at him.

"My dear, you've been on the island five days."

"It's been a long five days," she noted.

"You have a high opinion of yourself if you think you can get a man to sell a waterfront resort at a loss for you."

"Good," she said. She didn't want to be ransomed anyway. Still, it stung when he put it like that. "You had the resort. You got what you wanted. Why did you sell it back to them anyway?"

"My nephews work there. They grew up there. They love that eye sore of a resort. They would have hated me for bulldozing over their childhood."

"Again."

He glared at her and she wondered if she pushed him too far with that comment. "So I made a deal. I figured there was no way in hell the Kincaides could make a profit in a year's time. If they couldn't, I would raze the place and put up condos. My nephews wouldn't consider me the bad guy. It was a win-win situation."

"But you lost." Yeah, definitely not winning any brownie points with him.

"I did. I couldn't go back on my word for personal and professional reasons. Although, I managed to raise the selling price a bit more than previously agreed on." He smirked.

"So now you're trying to get it back by getting their licenses revoked and harassing them with legalities."

"I have an excellent lawyer." He snapped his fingers, and dessert and coffee was brought out.

Michaela argued to herself that even though Tetsuo was a douche, it didn't mean that she couldn't enjoy the crème brûlée.

"How would you like to work for me?" he asked.

"I have a job."

"I could set you up in your own law firm down here, after you pass the bar. Feed you some clients. What do you have waiting for you back in California? Your fiancé?"

Michaela blinked at him. If he wasn't such an evil bastard, she was being offered the gig of a lifetime. Her own firm? Instead of busting her ass to get to be partner, she'd be her own boss. Make her own hours. She shook herself out of the tempting day dream. Tetsuo was a smart man and she couldn't let her guard down.

"Is that why I'm here? So you can offer me a job? Why the gorgeous hotel room? I thought everything was booked for the surfing competitions this week."

Tetsuo was back to his fake smiles. "There are always rooms available. The fact that it's been five days and Amelia hasn't found you one should be a clue that the Palekaiko Resort is the armpit of Kaanapali. They can renovate as much as they want, but it's like putting lipstick on a pig. Every business owner there wants condos instead of that resort. And they're willing to help me obtain it."

"Seems a little unfair."

"Just think about my offer. Perhaps if you stayed in Maui longer, your fling with Marcus Kincaide could turn permanent. Perhaps you could influence him to consider another property. Maybe a coffee plantation upcountry? I think he'd make a better husband than Gerald Stone."

Pretty much anyone would at this point.

"As you noted, it's been less than a week," she said.

"I'm sure you'll find that I'm a very reasonable man."

"When you're getting what you want," Michaela countered.

He narrowed his eyes at her. "You may have noticed, the alternatives are not as pleasant."

"I will think about your kind offer." Her answer was hell no, but this room was pretty nice, and it could give her an opportunity to observe Tetsuo up close. She didn't trust him as far as she could throw him, though.

He got up from the table. After snapping his fingers, her cell phone was returned to her along with a key folio with one key card in it. "Take your time. When you're ready to return Amelia's car to her, just ring for the valet from the room and it will be outside the lobby by the time you get downstairs. Enjoy your stay."

Michaela snagged his untouched dessert before his servant could. They all trailed out of her room and shut the door.

Blissfully alone, she stared out into the ocean until it was too dark to see, tempted more than she'd like to admit by Tetsuo's offer.

Chapter Twelve

MICHAELA PARKED AMELIA'S CAR IN THE PARKING GARAGE and hung her keys on Amelia's peg behind the registration desk. Amelia had said to bring her laptop up to her room when she got back. She considered finding Hani or someone and getting them to do it because she didn't feel like talking about her day right now. It would be so easy to drop it off and then turn right around and take a cab back to Wailea, where room service and that big, beautiful bed awaited her. But the luau was going on full force, and she wandered outside to watch.

"You look like you need some advice," an older woman, with dark eyes stared up at her. She was dressed like a gypsy, with an island flair. She sat at a card table with a lacy tablecloth. Spread out in front of her were Tarot cards. The pin on her shirt said, Zarafina.

"How much?" Michaela asked, taking a seat.

"Ten dollars for ten minutes."

Michaela handed her the money.

"Is there something special you would like to ask? If there's romance in your future or a new job?"

She nodded. "Yeah, that sounds good."

Zarafina shuffled the cards, the flashy rings on her fingers catching the light of the torches. "Cut them."

Michaela did and felt a tiny frisson of energy spark when she did. Must be static electricity.

She dealt the cards with a practiced hand, doing a lot of "hmms" and "uh huhs." Michaela waited, hoping to hear a good story.

"I see a lover, a dark haired man."

She tried not to react. Marcus was blond.

"He's searching for you."

On the other hand, Gerald had dark, brown hair.

"He has a selfish purpose."

Michaela leaned forward in her seat in spite of herself. Definitely Gerald.

"He's going to cause trouble for you. There's a lot of trouble up ahead for you."

Michaela groaned. "That figures. Is there anything good?"

"Oh yes," she said. "The best. If the forces of evil are thwarted."

"Thwarting evil. Got it." Michaela rose out of her chair. She had been hoping for a "you're going to have fun, excitement and lots of sex before going back to work" type of reading. Heck, she would have settled for "you're going to meet a tall, blond man who will give you a great orgasm." Again. She sighed.

"Wait," the woman held out a hand.

"You must tell him the truth."

"Who?"

Zarafina looked at her. "You know who."

Ice tickled down Michaela's spine. First Tetsuo knowing all about her, and now this crazy gypsy woman.

"Don't let the consequences stop you."

"Honesty is the best policy." Michaela gave her a quick smile and then darted away.

That was weird.

She walked over to the building where the Kincaide's had their penthouse rooms and took the elevator up. She couldn't help compare the two resorts and tried not to hear the chugging of the elevator or the slight wobble and screech as it stopped.

Knocking on their door, she didn't get an answer. But Marcus opened his up. He scowled out until he saw her, and his face changed to a delighted smile.

"I wanted to return Amelia's laptop," she said. "She let me borrow it today." Her heart gave a little stutter when she saw him. Stupid heart.

"For what?"

"Checking email and stuff. Do you know where she is?"

"They're spending the night on the yacht."

Michaela grinned. "Good for them. Can I give it to you?"

He nodded. "Come in for a bit. Do you want some dinner?"

"No thanks. I already ate."

Marcus didn't move out of the doorway enough, so she had to brush up against him as she went by. It sent a flush of excitement through her.

"How's your head?" Michaela set the laptop down on an end table and turned back to scrutinize the wound.

"Good as new," he said.

It didn't look good as new, but it wasn't puffy or sore. "It still looks like it hurts."

"Worst part is I can't go in the water for a while."

"That is bad news." Because she couldn't help herself, she hugged him. "I was really worried about you."

His strong arms wrapped around her. "My head is tough. I've had worse." He stroked her back.

She leaned up on tiptoes and kissed him. His mouth was warm and soft. Michaela sighed as he licked and nibbled on her lips. He kissed like a dream. They were keeping it light, so she didn't drop her hand to his pants like she wanted to. She had to remember that the doctor said, no strenuous activity for a few days. When his hands went up her shirt, she backed away.

"What's wrong?" he asked.

She pointed to his head. "We need to take it easy until you're better."

"I said I was fine." Marcus took her hand and dragged her back into his arms. He placed her hand on his cock. She couldn't help but rub his hard length a few times before taking her hand away.

He let out a long, suffering sigh. "So what did you do today?"

"Went sightseeing." She gave a short laugh.

"Where did you go?"

"Wailea. Nice place."

He rubbed her back. She cuddled in closer to him, no longer wanting to go back to the Kaimana Resort no matter how pretty it was.

"Missed you today."

"What did you wind up doing?" she asked.

"Not a damned thing. I walked around a bit though to get some air. I was hoping to run into you. Why didn't you answer your cell?"

130

"Huh?" She pulled away from him to check her phone. There were five missed messages. Two from him. Two from Gerald, and one from Amelia. "Oh shit. I must have had it turned off. I'm sorry."

"It's okay. I was hoping to get a chance to talk to you about something." He took her hand and led her over to the couch.

She sat next to him. "Is this a serious conversation or can I stretch out?"

"Make yourself comfortable."

Kicking off her shoes, she lay down on the couch and draped her legs over his knees.

"Ticklish?" he asked, grabbing her feet and massaging them.

"Not even a little bit." She grinned at him and relaxed. "That feels good."

"If you want to get more comfortable, feel free. I can help you take your shorts off."

Her panties were already soaked from his kisses. If her shorts came off, she knew there would be strenuous activity.

"I'll keep that in mind."

Marcus stroked her leg. "I've been thinking about you and our circumstances."

"What about?" she asked, spreading her legs a little so he could reach higher. This was probably going to get out of control and she should leave. In a minute. Or two.

"I'm not sure how to say this, so I'm going to come right out with it. Please don't be offended."

"Uh oh," she said, wondering where this was going.

"I want to offer you a job."

You too? Almost popped out of her mouth before she clamped it shut.

"A job?" she gave a half grin, not sure if he was serious or not. "I figured you'd be asking me for one." She licked her lips and eyed his lap.

His eyes darkened. "Don't distract me."

Actually, that sounded like a really good idea. If she knelt between his legs, it wouldn't be too strenuous for him.

"We've been looking for a surf instructor and I think you'd be great at it. We've got a good salary, paid benefits, room and board."

Michaela pulled her feet away and sat up. A part of her actually considered it. If she was going to quit her job, hanging out at the beach all day sounded really nice. She gave a half laugh, so much for all those college loans and all-nighters studying. "That's really very generous of you. I'm not sure why you're offering me a job, though."

At least with Tetsuo, she knew it was a carrot versus the stick approach. He wanted her on his team if she found out something that could be used against him. Plus, he probably thought that it would yank Marcus' chain.

"Can we be honest with each other?" Marcus leaned in.

Michaela broke out in a cold sweat. The gypsy had told her to be honest. "Of course."

"Do you have a place to stay at nights?"

She nodded. It wasn't even a lie, as long as he didn't ask about Hani and Amelia helping her out.

"You're not really on vacation are you?"

That threw her. She cocked her head at him. "Yeah, I am. I'm here for two weeks. Then it's back to California."

Maybe, the little voice who was still considering Tetsuo's offer whispered.

"Where are you staying?"

"Wailea," she said, glad that she didn't have to lie to keep Hani and Amelia from getting in trouble. "Why are you asking me this?"

"I think you've hit some hard times and could use a helping hand."

"I'll admit I've had better weeks, but I'm okay. Really, you don't need to worry about me." She leaned in and kissed him. "You're a sweet man. But I don't want to work for you."

"Why not?"

She straddled his legs so they faced each other. His hands immediately went to her ass. "Because I'd rather do this."

"I'm worried about you," Marcus said. "You'd tell me if you were in trouble right?"

The gypsy woman's words flashed back at her. If she was right there was a lot of trouble coming.

"I would," she said, caressing his cheek. "I'm worried about you too. You made a powerful enemy."

"That's why you should answer your phone when I call you," he growled.

"Did you want to see me this afternoon?"

"I wanted to see all of you this afternoon." His hands went up her shirt again, and this time she let him play with her breasts.

133

She kissed him until, she was rubbing herself over his hard cock. Breathing heavily, she came up for air. "We can't do anything too strenuous until your head heals up."

"I'm fine," he insisted.

"But I'm only here for another week and a half, and I don't want to waste all of our time." She pulled her shirt over her head and unhooked her bra.

Marcus groaned. "Stay here tonight."

"If I do, we're going to tear the staples out of your head with our exertions. Am I right?"

"Who cares?" he muttered.

"I do." She leaned forward so the tips of her breasts brushed against the stubble on his face. Marcus took a nipple in his mouth and sucked on it.

Michaela groaned, "Yeah." Scooting up closer on his lap, she used his hardness to rub against her clit.

"Take off your shorts" he said. "I want to be inside of you."

"No," she said on a half moan. "No sex, until you're better."

He clasped her breasts together and took both of her nipples in his mouth.

"But that doesn't mean, we can't have a little fun tonight." She cried out again, putting her hands on his shoulders.

He was fully dressed, with his hands down the back of her shorts. Michaela got herself off on the hard ridge of his cock through his jeans while he lavished kisses and licks over her breasts.

She came, making sounds like an animal. Still in a frenzy, she slid down his body to her knees. Tearing open his jeans, she pulled them and his underwear down when he lifted his hips to help.

Michaela licked up his hard shaft, mesmerized by the feral look in his eyes.

"Come back up here." He crooked his finger.

Instead, she took him in her mouth and bobbed slowly up and down. Marcus held her head, but she didn't mind. His thumbs caressed her cheeks.

"You're so pretty," he said.

She took him deeper.

"Fuck," he groaned. "I can't last. It feels too damn good."

Michaela increased her pace. Gritting his teeth, Marcus shouted as he came. Smoothing her hair back with a shaky hand, he muttered, "Up here, now."

Climbing back on the couch, she kissed him. "How's your head?"

"Spinning," he sighed. "But in a good way."

Unbuttoning her shorts, Marcus kept kissing her.

"No over exerting yourself," she breathed, arching her neck as he licked down to her throat.

"I'm just going to move my two fingers," he said, pushing his hand down the front of her shorts.

Michaela moaned, spreading her legs wider for him.

"I can't wait to sink my cock into this wet heat."

He strummed his fingers against her clit until her head spun. They kissed faster, and she rode his fingers into a limb shaking orgasm.

Teasing her a little more, Marcus swallowed her little gasps as we went back to her breasts. "Stay with me, tonight." He tongued her nipples until she purred.

Michaela tangled her fingers in his hair and he hissed in pain.

"Oh, sorry! Sorry." She backed away from him.

"It's all right. Well worth it. Come back here." His slow grin was all sex and promise.

"Let me put my shirt on first."

"Where's the fun in that? He said, but he was tucking himself back in his pants. "Can I get you something to drink?"

"Why don't we go down to the tiki bar?" she said.

"Because the liquor's shit. I should know. I buy it."

She fastened her bra and pulled her T-shirt over her head. "I can get you the good stuff. I know people."

"Oh yeah?" Marcus tugged her to her feet and wrapped his arm around her. "We can always go to my yacht."

"You have a yacht?"

"Let's take a walk and I'll show you where she's anchored."

Chapter Thirteen

MARCUS WAS DRINKING A RUM AND COKE that was more rum than coke. Michaela had a Mai Tai in a tiki glass and from the way she was staggering into him, her drink was just as strong.

"Can't hold your liquor." He tsked tsked her.

"It's the sand." She giggled. "I can't get my footing."

"I'd carry you if I could, but with the rum and my head, I'd probably drop you."

"Are the shark signs still up?" she asked.

"I don't know. They shouldn't be."

"Do you think Tetsuo paid someone off to keep the signs up so that the tourists will get pissed?"

"I wouldn't put it past him. But he's screwing all the hotels on the strip, if he is. That takes some balls just to try to stick it up our ass."

"There are plenty of other beaches too. All he's doing is being annoying."

"Like a fly that needs to be swatted." But Marcus didn't want to talk about Tetsuo. He made his head hurt, even though the rum and Michaela had been the best medicine. "Tell me about yourself, beautiful. I want to know you."

"What do you want to know?" she asked, tugging him down on the sand at a safe distance from the pounding water.

"Everything. Start from the beginning. I was born and then what?" Marcus realized he was on his way to drunk, but it was a happy drunk, so he went with it. He probably shouldn't be drinking after his head injury, but he was already giving up sex with Michaela, he deserved a drink.

"I can't remember that far back. Sometimes I have a hard time remembering what I had for lunch."

"You're first memory, then." Marcus pulled her in front of him, sitting her between his legs. He wrapped his arms around her and buried his face in her hair. She smelled like sunshine and the ocean, like she was the embodiment of Hawaii for him. He'd never have met her if he was in New York. He'd still be dating gorgeous socialites who wouldn't want to surf for fear of breaking a nail.

"A birthday party. I think I was five. There was an ice cream cake with the chocolate crunchies inside."

"I love those," he said in her ear.

"My dad hired a clown."

"Creepy."

"Right? I wouldn't go near it. But my father took off work and spent the day with me. I think that was the last time he ever did."

"Did the clown scare him too?"

"Maybe," she nodded. "He owns his own business, Harris Industries in Malibu. As the CEO," she changed her voice to sound gruff and deep. "I have a lot of things on my plate. People depend on me for their jobs."

"If I didn't work so hard, you wouldn't have all these nice things," Marcus said in the same voice.

"You too, huh?"

"Mine's a politician. He was a Senator when we lived in Maryland. My mother's a photo journalist. They've been divorced for a few years now. She's in Costa Rica somewhere and he's working on his third trophy wife. We're not very close, but we email a few times a week."

"You seem close to your brother."

"He's an asshole," Marcus said without any rancor in his voice.

"It's obvious that he cares about you. He was worried about you taking your medicine this morning."

Marcus stiffened. "That's because it wasn't my medicine."

She tilted her head back. "They sent the wrong prescription?"

"No, it was another "fuck you" from Tetsuo." He rubbed her arms when goosebumps came over her flesh. Was he going to tell her the deep, dark, family secret? He was feeling good enough that his anxieties over it had faded. And after some sleep and some sweet kisses, Marcus wasn't obsessing over the pills anymore. His new obsession was currently in his arms.

"That's awful," Michaela said. "You could have gotten sick."

"Worse," he said. "I could have gotten re-addicted."

She tried to spin around, but he hugged her tighter. "No, it's easier if you're not looking at me. I don't have to see any judgment and you don't have to see my shame."

"I would never judge you."

His laugh was without humor. "Everyone else did."

She stroked his arms and leaned back against him. "You don't have to tell me if you don't want to."

"There's not much to tell. I tore my ACL playing football. The coach wanted me back ASAFP. I healed. Got surgery. All the time taking these little pills that made everything all better. I waited the minimum amount of time and I was back on the field."

"You're lucky you can still walk."

"I'm lucky I'm still here. Eventually, the doctors caught on and I couldn't get my prescriptions filled. So I took to the streets to find another supplier."

"How old were you?"

"Eighteen. Samuel was just entering high school. I was just leaving it. One of the kids had connections and I coasted there for a while. Then he told me that heroin had the same effect, but it was cheaper and easier to get."

"Oh no," she said.

"I went to the buy. But that stupid, little shit of a brother of mine followed me. I wasn't going to buy drugs with him looking on. So I dragged him home and told my parents I had a problem."

"Good for you."

"They told everyone that I had gotten into college early, and they shipped me away to rehab. I didn't have to stay. I was an adult, but they told me I'd be cut off without a cent if I didn't stay for the full year. So I spent my senior year in rehab."

"What?"

He nodded. "Brutal, but I got to hand it to them. It scared me straight. I never played football again. It's been over ten years and I usually don't take anything for pain. This week has been an exception."

"It certainly has." She was silent so long, he thought she fell asleep.

"My father wanted a boy," Michaela said. "He's got no use for women. He runs an industrial plant where men work on big machines and men sell his products and men come up with the marketing. Women are good for answering phones and such. So even though we had the money, he didn't think it was a good idea for me to go to college."

"What?" Marcus snorted. "What century is he from?"

"So he refused to pay for it. He wanted me to find a rich husband instead."

"What did your mother have to say about that?"

"Darling, please don't shout. Mommy has a headache. Can you fix her a nice martini? There's a good girl." Michaela drawled on in a high pitched voice.

"What did you do?"

"He forgot to take away my credit card. So I charged the first two semesters before I maxed it out. By that time, I had a full time job and was able to get some loans to help out."

"Did he ever offer to pay for some of it?"

Michaela shook her head.

"Are you still paying it off?"

She laughed. "Almost."

"So you're from California, huh?"

"Born and raised."

"That's a long way from New York," he said. Another reason for him to consider making the move to Hawaii permanent?

"It's only four hours from Cali," she said.

Maybe Samuel was right and it was time to get out of Hawaii. He could find a nice hotel to buy out in California. But it was nights like these that made him wish he could stay forever. There was something magical about this place. It had brought her into his life.

"Michaela, I was serious about the job."

"I know. I have a job back in California that makes me a lot of money, though. And although I'm tempted, really tempted, to take you up on your offer, I didn't put myself through school to teach surfing. After the novelty wore off, I'd be bored."

Marcus knew the feeling. That's why going to back to New York was still on the table, but he was still trying to convince himself that's what he really wanted.

"I need to make sure you have a place to eat and sleep."

"Why would you think I didn't?"

He sighed. "Holt told me about finding you in the dumpster."

"Oh for Pete's sake, is that what this is about?"

"You lied to him. You said you lost your ring on the beach. You were with me all day."

This time he let her turn so he could look into her eyes. Instead of guilt, though, he saw outrage. "I lied so I didn't look like a bigger idiot." She sighed. "I was looking for my ring. It turned out that it didn't get thrown out by mistake, but I hadn't known that at the time."

"Why were you looking through our trash?" he asked. Had Tetsuo send her to investigate the contractors?

"I lost it on the property. I was desperate."

She was holding something back.

"So where is the ring now?"

"It's in a safe place."

"Why aren't you wearing it?"

Michaela shook her head vehemently. "Never again. That ring is cursed."

"Now that sounds like a story I want to hear."

She looked up at him with her beautiful brown eyes and there were tears in them.

142

"Baby, what's wrong?" he asked.

"I want to tell you that story. But not tonight. I'm too tired. I just want to go to bed."

"Come upstairs with me," he asked.

"Not tonight." She gently touched his head. "A few more days and I will."

"We don't have a lot of time," he said.

"We might," she said cryptically, standing up and brushing sand off her.

She held out a hand for him and he considered tugging her back down on top of him and recreating the kiss *From Here to Eternity*. But truth be told, he was pretty tired too.

"Getting hurt sucks," he said.

"I'm glad it wasn't worse."

He walked her out to the lobby and handed her into the cab.

"Where to?"

"Wailea Marriot," she said, looking down into her lap.

"Can I see you tomorrow?" he asked.

"Yeah," she said. "Call me when you get up?"

He watched the car pull away before he pulled out his phone. "Wailea Marriot." While his phone dialed the number, he still stared off in the direction she left.

"Hi, I want to send flowers to one of your guests. Michaela Harris."

"What room is she in?"

"I forgot, but if I send the flowers to the desk would you be able to get them to her room?"

He heard typing. "I'm sorry I don't have a guest by that name."

Marcus' heart sunk. He hadn't thought so. When she came firing into the lobby yesterday morning, she hadn't gotten out of a cab. She came via Kaanapali Beach, which means she was staying close by.

He told her his deepest secret. And she fucking lied to him in return.

Chapter Fourteen

MICHAELA WOKE UP FEELING GUILTY IN her exquisite bed, in her luxurious hotel room. She shouldn't be here. She, more than anyone else, knew nothing was ever free. Still, Amelia promised her a hotel room tomorrow. She could slum it another night here. Tossing back the comforter on the bed, she called Marcus.

"Good morning," she said into his voicemail. "Let's go on an adventure. I'm hopping in the shower now. Give me a call when you get up."

Except he hadn't called after her shower. Nor after breakfast or even after she walked around the beach for a bit. Maybe, his head was still bothering him. She didn't want to keep leaving messages though, so she called the Palekaiko Resort. Hani answered, but he hadn't seen him all day either. He said he'd ask around to see if he had breakfast delivered yet, and would call her back.

Michaela changed into her swimsuit and pulled a sundress over it. She'd take a cab ride over to Kaanapali and see if he was around. If not, she'd go shopping at Whaler's Village. Hani called back while she was in the cab and said that Amelia saw him earlier and other than being in a foul mood, Marcus seemed to be doing all right.

Michaela couldn't figure out why he wasn't calling her back. Had she misread the signals? Was he mad because she wouldn't go back to the room with him? Because she didn't have anything else to do, she listened to Gerald's voice mails.

HI BABE, I SAW THAT YOU CALLED BUT EVERYTHING WAS ALL GARBLED. CALL ME BACK WHEN YOU GET THIS.

So much for being rescued. It was a good thing she knew how to rescue herself. She played the second one.

Michaela sighed. This wasn't how it was supposed to go. She wasn't supposed to feel guilty for stranding the idiot at the airport.

"I changed my mind," she said to the cab driver. "Can you drop me off at Whaler's Village instead?"

"Shoots." The driver shrugged and let her out in front of the shopping mall.

She found a secluded bench and called Gerald back. Her gut churned when he answered the phone.

"Finally," he said and there was a touch of annoyance that set her right on the edge. "Your dad says hi."

"He's there now?"

"No, I had dinner with him last night."

"Did he punch you in the face?" she asked, hoping and yet not hoping.

"What? No, of course not. We talked. Got a few things straightened out."

"I'm so glad," she drawled.

"How does a fall wedding sound to you?"

She could not believe the gall of this man. "Why? Do you want leave me standing at the altar for a second time?"

"Don't be ridiculous," he said in a cold tone that stiffened her spine. "I told you what happened."

"No, Gerald. You really didn't. You gave me a bullshit line about being stressed about clients and you texted your sister that you couldn't go through with it because you didn't love me."

146

Michaela caught a few people staring at her and she made an effort to lower his voice.

She let the silence grow, knowing that he used it as a technique in court to get witnesses to say more than they should. She felt a flare of victory when he spoke first.

"I've changed my mind," he said, at last.

"So have I. I didn't think that this needed to be said. I thought it was obvious. Let me make it clear, since there's obviously a disconnect somewhere. We're through. There is no you and I. We are no longer dating. I don't even like you much, right now. Even if I did, I don't want to go back to the type of relationship where you couldn't give me the courtesy to tell me that you didn't want to get married before I humiliated myself in front of all of my co-workers and our families."

Michaela realized that she didn't say friends. How sad was that? Everyone at the wedding had been all of Gerald's friends. Her bridesmaids had been Gerald's family. She had been working so hard to get out of debt and chasing that elusive partner carrot that they dangled in front of her nose that she forgot about everything else in life. Like friends, and surfing, and drinking on a beach late at night with a handsome man who kissed like it was his job.

"You're not over that yet? It's been a week."

Now, it was her turn to seethe in silence.

"I'm sorry," he said. "That was a bad joke."

"A part of me will never get over that," she said.

"Stop being so dramatic."

"I was being honest. Do you think that I like how much power that gives you over me? That I'll never stand in a church in a wedding dress ever again because of you."

"You can do it in September," Gerald groaned in frustration.

"No, I won't," Michaela groaned back at him.

"Fine. Be difficult. We'll get married at the town hall."

"I'm not sure I can make this anymore plain to you. I'm not marrying you. I'm no longer your girlfriend. You can give my key back to my father. If he's willing to overlook the money he paid for my dress, the limo, and the reception, I'll Fed Ex your ring back to you. If not, I'm holding it as insurance that you'll reimburse him in a timely manner."

"Michaela, you can't do that."

"Why the hell not? You don't love me and I don't love you. In fact, I've met someone down here." Someone who hasn't called me back all day, but she was sure there was a good reason for that.

"You're having an affair?"

"I prefer the term vacation fling." He didn't have to sound so surprised about it. "And I'd rather be with him than with you, so save yourself the trouble and stay home. Or come out and have a nice vacation. It's a big island. Just don't call me. We have nothing more to say to each other."

"Wait! Don't hang up." He sighed. "You're right. I should have told you. I'm sorry I didn't have the balls to tell you before the wedding."

Finally, an apology. A week later and a lifetime too late.

"I honestly thought I could go through with it," Gerald continued. "We are compatible in every way. You're intelligent and hardworking. You understand my schedule. You don't expect roses or candles or any of that romantic nonsense."

"I need to raise my expectations," she whispered. But he continued on as if he hadn't heard.

"Then Brittany called and we had sex the night before our wedding."

"After you left me? You cheated on me?" That stung too. She had been faithful to him. She never would have banged her ex while she was still with Gerald. What a prick!

"I'm not proud of it. But it happened, and I couldn't marry you when I still wanted her. We were still in bed when I should have been at the church."

Michaela winced at that image. "So, let me guess. She went back to the bass player? Again."

He chuffed out a laugh. "No, she moved in with me."

"Okay, I'm officially confused." Michaela looked up into the sky for guidance, but all she saw was fluffy clouds and a pretty blue expanse that she wanted to get lost in.

"I've got business in Maui next week. Let's talk about this in person."

That son of a bitch had been planning on working on their honeymoon all along. She felt like screaming in frustration. Brittany was welcome to him.

"It's got to do with the Harris Industries and Stone Mechanics merger, doesn't it? That's what my father was talking with you about."

"I looked at the contracts. It's a lucrative deal for both of them. But your father is being really stubborn about keeping the business in the family."

"Then he can marry you." She hung up and turned off her phone. Michaela was surprised to find that she was shaking and on the verge of tears. This completely sucked. She calmed down a bit, walking towards the Palekaiko Beach Resort. The water was like glass, not even a chance of a curl today. But at least the shark

149

warning signs were gone and people were back in the water enjoying themselves. Samuel was swaying in his hammock, so she veered off to say hello.

"Howzit, Dude," she said.

"If it isn't the *wahine* with the teeny bikini. Want a beer?"

"It's not even noon."

"It's five o'clock somewhere."

He had a point. She could use a drink, but she needed the ocean more.

"You looking for my *bruddah*?"

She rolled her eyes at his pidgin. "Nah, actually I was looking to do some snorkeling and I hear you're the man to see about that." Michaela never was the clingy type and she wasn't about to start now. Marcus was a busy man, and she was on vacation.

He nodded. "Amelia told me to hook you up. Have you ever been snorkeling before?"

"Yeah, lots of times. I'm more of a surfer girl, though."

"Not today, you're not. Not here anyway."

"I noticed. Maybe the wind will pick up later." She looked wistfully out into the blue water, itching to dive in and forget this morning ever happened.

"It's possible. They just gave us the all clear this morning, so you won't have to worry about sharks."

"I always worry about sharks. But I'm glad they've decided to leave us alone today. The kind on two legs as well as the ones with the big teeth."

He looked up at her quizzically. "You okay?"

"I will be."

Dude nodded, and set her up with fins, mask and a tube. "You want a vest?" he asked, indicating one of the inflatable ones.

Michaela shook her head. "No. I want to get down low and explore."

"All right, but if you ever go out by Molokini or Lanai, you wear one of these." He shook it at her.

"Yeah, maybe I'll take a tour out there tomorrow." She should look into the wetsuit that had the inflatable on the back, especially if she was craving the bigger waves. There was an air canister in one brand in case she was held under water, she could activate it and it would float her up. But that wasn't a concern for today. She really wanted to go back to Ho'okipa, but she was afraid to go alone.

"Marcus can take you." For a moment, she thought he meant Ho'okipa.

"Are you volunteering him? That won't be any fun. He can't get his wound wet yet."

Samuel shrugged. "He's in a good mood. We got news that we're completely booked for the next two years."

Michaela grinned. "That's awesome. Good for you guys."

Samuel gave her a strange look. "Yeah, it is good. We also found a way to keep Tetsuo off our backs."

"That's good to hear," she said, distractedly. Hopefully, Amelia was able to run down some of the leads she gave her. "I'll stop by later and give Amelia my congratulations." She headed toward Black Rock.

"*Wahine*?"

"Yeah, Dude?"

"Since you're not wearing the vest, don't go around the point. The current is bad. People have drowned."

She shuddered. "Thanks for the warning."

"Yeah." He was still frowning when she put on the fins and checked her mask. She wondered if he knew why Marcus wasn't calling. But she wasn't going to ask. Either he'd call or he wouldn't. There was too much ocean out there to worry about Gerald or Marcus.

Michaela walked in until it was over her head and then swam on the surface to get her bearings. The bottom was beautiful sand and the water crystal clear. As she swam out deeper, she saw schools of colorful fish. Testing her air tube, she took a practice dive to the bottom and let the soft powder sand slip through her fingers. Gently, she glided back up to the top and blew water out of the mouthpiece. It was fine.

What she liked most about being underwater when she wasn't being tossed around like a ragdoll, was the silence. It helped clear out all the voices in her head that whispered awful things like she should take Gerald up on his offer for a quickie wedding at City Hall. It would make her father happy. The merger would make everyone involved a lot of money. She didn't have anyone who would really care if she got married. As long as she knew it was temporary, why not cave into her father's demands like she always did?

Michaela blew out more water from the tube when she surfaced and those thoughts went out the tube as well. She didn't need her father's approval anymore. If he wanted to risk his financial future to run her life, that was his mistake.

Diving deeper this time, she hugged the rock wall and followed some colorful fish that she had only seen online and in books. Michaela wished she had the forethought to have brought a

152

camera. Maybe when she went to Molokini she'd bring one. She floated close to the curve of the rock to see some sea turtles, but she could feel a change of temperature in the water and the current pulled at her. Michaela didn't want to ever leave, but she was getting tired. It had probably been a few hours.

Swimming sideways as she got closer to the surface, the waves were starting to roll in stronger. The wind must have kicked up. She dove down deep, skimming closer to the curve in the rock. A commotion in the water behind her made her turn. She supposed it was too good to last to have this all to herself.

She was surprised to see Samuel in the water and he was waving her to come back to shore. A sliver of dread passed over her at the intense look in his eyes. He held out a hand to her. She waved him off and followed him. Was something wrong with Marcus? Samuel sped through the water, using clean swift strokes. Looking over her shoulder, she didn't see anything alarming. But that didn't mean there wasn't.

"Shark sighting," Samuel said when they were standing in the water.

A wave crashed her off her feet, but Michaela rolled with it and was glad for the push to shore. Sitting down on the beach, she tugged off her flippers while Samuel made a more dignified exit.

"Again?" Michaela refused to let her fear show, but she scanned the water intently.

He shrugged. "I didn't see it. No one has, but the DLNR just posted signs to close the beach."

She wondered if somehow Tetsuo was behind this just to break balls. "I'm glad I got in some snorkeling and that the biggest thing I saw was an eel."

The little Zodiac boats zoomed around, getting people in and patrolling the waters until everyone was out.

153

Walking back with him to his hammock, Michaela said, "Thanks for coming to get me."

"Not a problem. Want that beer now?"

Shaking her head, she gathered her things. "No, I'm going to see if I can catch some waves on the North Shore once I dry off enough."

She'd go back to Ho'okipa and damn anyone who tried to intimidate her off the waves.

"With Marcus?" He raised an eyebrow.

Michaela gave him a grim smile. "Nope. Haven't heard from him today."

He gave her a shaka. "Pretty girl like you shouldn't be alone."

"Preach." She winked at him and wandered until she found an abandoned beach chair.

Laying back, Michaela closed her eyes and thought it probably would have been a good idea to have brought sun block and a book. Well, she wouldn't be here that long. Just enough to dry off. As she was flipping through Facebook, Marcus called.

"Hey," she answered. "How's your head this morning?"

"Better. How was your night?"

"I slept like a baby." Today's going rather shitty, though. But she took in a cleansing breath before she said that to him.

"I'm tied up with work. I've got conference calls all day with our lawyer." Marcus said lawyer like most people say traffic.

"I know how much you enjoy that," she smiled sadly.

"It looks like we finally have something to nail Tetsuo to the wall with."

"Yeah, Dude mentioned that. Good for you."

"When did you talk to my brother?"

"About five minutes ago. I went snorkeling by Black Rock this morning."

"There were five tiger sharks sighted on the beach. You were in the water? They closed the beach." His voice was sharp with alarm.

"All I saw was an eel and some pretty fish." Michaela tried to sound light hearted. Five sharks? She blew out a breath. "Dude came and got me before I got into trouble."

"Are you here now?"

"Yup, sunning myself in a lounge chair. Want to come down and take a break with me?" Michaela wouldn't keep him long, but it would be nice share a kiss or two. She could really use a hug.

"I wish I could."

"Yeah, I understand. Meetings."

A part of her knew she was being unfair. She was on vacation. He was working.

"But I was wondering if you would be interested in an early dinner?"

Her heart lightened a little bit at that. "Yeah, I'd like that." Then, because she couldn't help twisting the knife a bit, she said, "I was heading out to do some surfing today. I'm not sure where I'll be. What time are you going to be free?"

"Why don't I pick you up at your hotel? Call me when you get back."

Michaela winced. She didn't want to admit to him she was staying at Tetsuo's hotel, not when tomorrow she'd be checking in here. Maybe she could go to Lahaina Beach instead and meet him at a local restaurant. "It's not a problem. There's no sense in making you come all that way. I can hang around here. Lahaina might be open."

"How about five at Leilani's then?"

"Sounds good," she said. Maybe she could get in a few waves after all.

Chapter Fifteen

MICHAELA POUNDED ON JOELY'S DOOR, shampoo stinging her eyes. She was going to be late for her date. Of course, she had spent too much time at Lahaina Harbor this afternoon. She had rented a board and rode waves with a bunch of nice people. No signs of sharks or any other weird activity, so she spent a calming and exhilarating day in the ocean.

"My water shut off mid shower," she said when Joely let her in. It had been easier to go back to her room here than to make the trek to Wailea. Besides, tomorrow was Sunday and she could move into her room once somebody checked out. She'd grab her bags in Wailea tomorrow morning, tell Tetsuo to shove his offer, and start her vacation for real.

Joely opened the bathroom door. "I can't believe your luck."

"Yeah, you and me both. I've got a hot date tonight with Marcus at Leilani's, and I don't want to meet him looking like this."

"A towel *is* a little casual for Leilani's. My bathroom is your bathroom," she said.

"Thanks." Michaela hopped into the shower and rinsed off her hair. After she got off the phone with Marcus, she had headed over to Whaler's Village and spent way too much money on a sexy, Louis Vuitton dress and some strappy sandals that were more for show than walking. She dumped the bags in her room at Palekaiko before taking a cab to Lahaina to surf.

Tonight was going to be her first real date in longer than she could remember. Gerald's idea of date night was takeout Chinese and Netflix. There was nothing wrong with that, but it would have been nice to go out once in a while. Normally, they were too tired to even make it to the movie.

Was that where it all went wrong?

As she was putting on the last touches of makeup, she heard raised voices from the other room.

"What's up?" she asked, poking her head out.

Joely was standing in her living room with her arms akimbo. Holt was looming over her.

"I was just telling Holt, here, that you and I were going out tonight, and it was easier for you to shower here." Joely turned to look at me and made exaggerated facial expressions.

Yeah, I get it. Cheez it, it's the cops.

"Is there a problem?" Michaela asked, stopping herself before she added "officer" after it.

"No problem. Where are you heading?" he asked politely.

"Why?" Michaela asked.

"Just curious."

"We're going to take a walk and see who has the best entertainment tonight. Do you know who's playing at the Hula Grill?" Joely asked.

Holt shook his head, still giving Michaela the fishy eyeball.

She shrugged at him and went back to finish her makeup. Joely and Holt talked for a few minutes, but she couldn't hear what they were saying. After the door closed, Joely came in the bathroom, madder than a hornet.

"I swear, he's part blood hound. He wanted to know who was in my shower."

"Sounds like he's jealous," Michaela said, hiding a smile.

"More like he thinks he's the Hawaiian Sherlock Holmes." She crossed her arms over her chest. "Now, I've got to get all gussied up and try not to crash your date or he'll get suspicious."

"I'm sorry," Michaela said.

Joely sighed. "No, it's all right. I'm not mad at you. I'm just aggravated at him. Give me a few minutes to get ready. I'll walk you over to Leilani's and then I'll fade away into the crowd."

"You're the best," Michaela said, and meant it.

"I want to hear all the juicy details about the *Kahuna*. And if you can get the stick out of his ass, we'll all be grateful."

Michaela laughed. "It's just dinner." But she hoped for a little more.

"Uh huh." Joely left to get dressed.

"It's not like I can take him back to my room," Michaela said, shouting over the blow dryer.

"He's got plenty of places to take you to."

Michaela hoped so. She really did.

Joely was ready by the time Michaela declared her hair was good enough. Being so thick and long, it would take forever to dry so she just put it into a French braid.

"That's a cute dress," Michaela said. Joely wore a white halter dress that showed lots of cleavage and was split up the sides.

"I figured, if I was going out, I was going to do it right. Here," she slipped a pretty ceramic flower on a hair clip over her right ear. "Makoa's sister makes these. This means you're looking for love."

"I'm not sure it's love I'm looking for."

She put one over her own right ear. "If not love, then maybe just a good time."

"I like how you think," Michaela said. Love didn't seem to be in the cards for her anyway. Hot sex, on the other hand, could be on the menu tonight—if Marcus' got the okay from his doctor to return to normal activities.

When they stepped outside, Holt was leaning up against a palm tree, waiting for them. He had changed into khakis and a polo shirt that showed off his massive chest and arms.

"I was heading over to Hula Grill, myself. Georgie and the Mangos are playing. Mind if I walk with you?" His gaze focused on Joely's flower, but he didn't mention it.

"Sure." Joely shrugged, and together they walked along the stone path by the beach.

"I'm Holt," he said, holding his hand out. "I don't think we were properly introduced the other night when you were in the dumpster."

"Michaela," she said, taking it.

He turned her hand over. "You're not wearing your ring?"

Michaela snatched her hand back. "My fingers swell in the heat."

"How do you know Joely?" he asked.

"We met a few days ago while surfing," Michaela said.

Holt shot Joely a look. "You didn't go to the Dumps, did you?"

She blew out a long, aggravated sigh. "No, we were at Honolua Bay."

"The waves were great, but then the beach got a little crowded." Michaela shrugged. "I'm looking forward to going back again."

"You should see if you can get to Oahu if you're looking for hot action," he said.

"Maybe I will."

"Where are you staying? They might be able to hook you up with a tour."

He was smooth. Michaela had to give him that. Joely shot her an alarmed look, but Michaela faced down worse prosecutors in court. "That's a great idea," she said, not answering his question.

Holt smiled, but she wasn't fooled. He knew she was on to him. "So how long are you here for?"

"Another week," she said. "Any suggestions on where to go?"

"If you want to do some body surfing, D.T. Fleming Beach is a good place," he said.

"Watch out for the rip currents," Joely said.

"You're a good swimmer," Holt said. "I heard you saved that boy that was snorkeling the other day."

Michaela shook her head. "That was Marcus. I just tried to get him on my surf board."

"Still, it was a good thing."

His frank words embarrassed her, and she looked away. He seemed a nice guy. She couldn't wait until tomorrow when she didn't have to pretend where she was living anymore. They walked on in silence for a few minutes. It was a beautiful night, but her feet were starting to hurt her in the sandals. She had only a vague idea where Leilani's was, but she could hear guitar music from up ahead.

"That's the Hula Grill," Joely said. "Leilani's is the next restaurant over."

"Who has the best malasadas?" Michaela asked the important question.

Joely and Holt looked at each other in confusion. "They don't have malasadas," Joely said. "But don't miss the Hula pie. It's got macadamia nut ice cream, cookies and hot fudge."

That didn't sound like it sucked.

"Or the pono pie if you want to try breadfruit and coconut."

"I'm on a mission," Michaela said. "I want to try all the malasadas in Maui. Who makes the best?"

Holt smiled. "My auntie," he said at the same time as Joely said, "Zippy's."

He looked at her askance. They bickered for a few minutes, throwing out restaurant names like they were in a duel. Michaela mentally made notes of some of the places they mentioned.

"I'll get my auntie to make a batch and you'll see," he said.

They came up on the Hula Grill. "What are you drinking, ladies?" Holt asked.

"Gosling and diet coke," Joely said.

Holt raised his eyebrow at Michaela. "Me too," she said.

When he shouldered his way to the bar, Joely pulled her through the crowd and pointed. "Go down that way and you should see Leilani's on your left."

"What about Holt and the drinks?"

"I'll drink both and keep him busy. Now, go before he looks over here."

"Are you sure you'll be all right with him?"

Joely smiled a little sadly. "Yeah, I'll keep him entertained until your trail is cold. At least I got some free booze out of it, right?"

Michaela hugged her. "You're the best."

Joely blushed. "You owe me details."

"Deal."

Michaela made sure Holt still had his back to them, and then she darted through the crowds. She found Leilani's easily. She'd actually passed it this afternoon when she was dress shopping. Marcus was sitting at an outside table at the front of the restaurant. Michaela had a moment to study him. He was staring out at the ocean, his green eyes faraway and his expression solemn. The wound on his forehead looked a little better.

He was dressed in a crisp linen suit. Michaela was glad she put the extra effort in her new outfit, even if her feet were killing her now. Marcus held a glass of white wine in his hand, and when he took a sip, he noticed her standing there. Standing up, he came to the edge of the railing.

"You can walk around there to get out here. Just tell him you're with me."

"Okay," she said and hurried inside, suddenly eager to sit down and have a glass of wine.

He held out the seat next to him, so they could both look out at the water. Of course, that meant her leg was pressed up next to him and his arm draped over the back of her chair.

"Do you like pinot grigio?" He trailed his fingers over her upper arm. Her nipples hardened in reaction.

"Yeah," Michaela said, a little breathless from being so near him. He smelled like coconut and spice.

Filling up her wine glass, he said, "I took the liberty of ordering for us. I ordered a bunch of tapas so we could have a taste of everything, but if you're really hungry we can order dinners."

"No, that sounds good." Michaela was surprised she was so nervous. After all, they had practically slept together. This was just dinner.

"Great." He clicked glasses with her. "I'm glad you're here."

"Me too."

The waitress jumped in during the awkward silence with the first set of dishes. A beet salad with goat cheese and macadamia nuts was placed in front of them, as well as a small tray of shrimp in lemon butter.

Michaela tried to eat daintily, but that was never her gig. Soon she was leaning back in her chair, sipping wine while Marcus finished his first course. She started to relax, really relax for the first time since she got to Maui.

After the second glass of wine, she was lulled by the beauty of the ocean. As she watched the waves roll in, she realized she didn't give a shit about Tetsuo Hojo's nonsense, Gerald's continuing douche baggery, or that she didn't have a hotel room that either came with huge strings or could get her friends in trouble.

"Aside from surfing and dodging sharks, what else are you planning on doing in Maui?"

You.

Kicking off her shoes under the table, Michaela stretched and said instead, "I suppose I should do some more sightseeing, but all I want to do is surf."

"Me too."

"It's weird. I used to surf all the time in California, but I stopped. Too many grown up things to do. Now, that I've found the waves again. I'm afraid that when I go back, I won't get back out on the board."

"Because of the sharks?" he frowned.

"No." She shook her head. "I've got a healthy fear of sharks, but they're a part of the ocean. It's like I'm different here. I don't know if that sounds silly, but it's more than being on vacation."

"No, I get it. Maui has a way of getting in your blood. There's no place like it."

"You said before that you owned a chain of hotels in New York, right?"

He nodded.

"Are you ever going back?" Michaela knew she didn't want to work with Tetsuo, but was she crazy to think she could start her own firm here?

"Trying to get rid of me?" Marcus said with a smile that didn't reach his eyes.

She shook her head. "No, you know what I mean. You said it yourself the night we met. It's hard being so far away. Would it be easier if you were on the East Coast? What's keeping you in Maui?"

He gave a half laugh. "I ask myself that almost daily. The answer is mainly the obvious. It's January in New York. I'll wait out the winter here, and then go back in the spring. I stayed last year because of the trouble we were having with Tetsuo."

"He's a piece of work." She held out her glass for another refill. "How did everything go today with your lawyer?"

"Another bottle?" he asked. His phone rang. He glanced at it and ignored it.

"I'm not driving," she said.

Flagging the waitress down, he ordered another bottle of the pinot grigio.

"You can see my sailboat a little better here." He pointed out in the water. She could barely see the outline of it last night in the dark, but it had looked big.

"Holy crap, that's huge. No wonder you call it a yacht."

"If you'd like, we can have a night cap there."

Michaela smiled. She liked how he thought. "How would we get there?"

"We'd take a Zodiac."

"In shark infested waters?" she arched an eyebrow at him. "Last time I checked the caution signs were still up."

"They very rarely attack the boats." His phone beeped a few times. He was either getting a text or voicemail. She could see the effort it was taking him not to answer it. He got points for that. Gerald would have taken the calls and texts.

"I saw the movie, *Jaws*. You're going to need a bigger boat. No thanks."

"If you're chicken..." Marcus trailed off.

Michaela refused to rise to the bait, no matter how much her competitive nature wanted her to. "Bawk Bawk," she said mildly.

The next course was crispy wontons and fried spring rolls with a variety of sauces. Since they were sharing this plate, Michaela reined herself in. The food was the best she had tasted in a long while, although that could be the setting and the company.

"What do you do when you're not surfing?" he asked.

Michaela chewed while she thought up an answer. Now that she knew how deep his hatred of lawyers went, she certainly wasn't going to own up to being one. Unfortunately, that left her with lying and she didn't want to do that.

"I'm trying to find myself." She winced. "I hate how new-agey that sounds. What I mean is I want to start enjoying my life instead of just waking up, going to work, and going to bed. Wash, rinse, repeat. I think that might be what went wrong with Gerald. It got boring."

She hadn't realized her hand was on his thigh until he tensed.

"Gerald is your ex?"

She nodded.

"You're still not over him?"

"Does it matter?" Michaela asked.

"I don't want you thinking of someone else when you're with me, that's all." He said with a light tone, but there was something almost feral behind his eyes.

She shrugged. "Try harder to keep my attention, then." And then stuck out her tongue to take the sting out of it.

He laughed. "I'll keep that in mind."

"How about you? What do you do when you're not bitching about the servers being down or soothing local bureaucrats?"

His phone rang again as if on cue. She took pity on him. "You can answer that if you want."

"I don't want to."

"Then turn it off," Michaela suggested.

"I can't." He grinned. "It's worse if I can't see who's calling. I like to work. It's easy and I enjoy what I do. I've been trying to decide if I want to embrace the *aloha* lifestyle or get back to New York and go balls to the wall again."

"Which do you like better?"

"Both have their appeal. I have a hard time letting go and getting my head out of my spreadsheets. But right now? I'd like nothing more than to be in a hammock with you."

She bit her lip and made her decision. "I'd rather be in a bed."

His face lost his teasing expression and was replaced with an intensity that made her wonder if she said the wrong thing.

"Good," he said.

She leaned in for another one of his devastating kisses, but the waitress interrupted them before his lips touched hers.

"Are you ready for dessert, Mr. Kincaide?" she asked.

Laughter danced in his eyes for a moment. "Definitely. Can we get two cups of Kona?"

The coffee and dessert came out and Michaela couldn't believe her eyes. There was a pile of little fried doughnuts. Malasadas.

"Joely said they didn't have malasadas on the menu," she said.

Marcus shrugged. "I asked the chef if he would make an exception. The ones rolled in choke sugar don't have any filling in them. But the other ones are filled with dobash."

"Dobash?"

"Chocolate cream."

Yeah, he was definitely getting laid tonight.

"What type of sugar is choke sugar?"

Marcus grinned self consciously. "That means there's just a lot of it."

She tilted her head. "Like I just ate *choke ono grindz*?"

"*Shoots*." He winked at her.

"See, you can lighten up."

"You make me feel that way." He picked up a chocolate malasada and offered it to her.

She opened her mouth and bit down, taking half of the little tidbit. He popped the other half in his mouth, licking the cream off his finger. "So what's the obsession with the malasadas anyway?"

Michaela sighed. "I'm going to tell you the story, but you have to promise me one thing."

"Sure."

"At the end of it, you and I are going back to your suite and have mind blowing, gravity defying sex all night long."

Marcus choked on his doughnut.

"You all right?" she asked.

"Check please," he called over his shoulder. "Talk fast." He grinned at her.

"I don't have to tell it to you at all," Michaela said, helping herself to one without the cream. It literally melted on her tongue, the sugar mixing with the airy dough. She closed her eyes in bliss.

"I have a feeling it's an important story." He sipped his coffee.

She was about to add milk to hers when he stopped her. "Have you ever had a hundred percent Kona?"

"No."

"Try it black first," he said.

"But I hate black coffee."

"You like coffee, right?"

Michaela picked up the cup and sniffed. It smelled great. "I can't get through a Monday without it, but I don't really enjoy it."

"Try a sip," he said with a knowing smile.

Why not? She did and frowned as a bunch of different flavors hit her tongue. "It's like tasting a wine. I can taste chocolate and a burnt caramel, but it's not sweet. Does that make any sense?"

"Yeah, if you want to doctor it up now, go ahead. But I wanted you to experience it in its purest form."

She looked at him through her lashes. "You're one of those coffee freaks, aren't you?"

"If I fell on a reef, I'd bleed coffee."

Michaela added cream and sugar, even though she knew he was a little disappointed. He let her eat one more malasada with her coffee before leaning in. "The story?"

Wiping the sugar from her mouth, she took another bracing sip of the coffee. Here goes nothing. "We're still going back to your room, right?"

"Even if the resort caught on fire," he promised.

"Okay." She heaved out a sigh, but chickened out on telling him the whole story. "I've been on a diet for about six months and every Monday a co-worker would bring in doughnuts and leave them in the break room. They're my kryptonite. I became obsessed with them. I went online to find out what doughnuts were available in Maui and came across these Portuguese delights. I made a vow that once I got here, I would eat them until I couldn't look at another doughnut without getting sick."

"Why were you on a diet?"

It figured he would pick up on that.

"And why would it bother me so much that I'd no longer want to kiss you."

Michaela stared into the bottom of her empty coffee cup. Well, here goes nothing. He wanted the whole story. He got the whole story. The fortune teller's words echoed in her head. *You must tell him the truth*

"I was supposed to get married a week ago today. Gerald left me at the altar."

Emotions flashed through his face: shock, disbelief, rage and then with trepidation he asked, "Why are you here in Maui?"

"It's my honeymoon."

Chapter Sixteen

MARCUS WAS STUNNED AND FOR THE first time in a long while, he was speechless. Michaela shifted nervously in her seat. He couldn't believe anyone would be so stupid, so vile to leave a beautiful woman waiting for him to show up at her wedding.

"You must be heartbroken," he said, clearing his throat. Only a grade-A schmuck would take advantage of a woman who had been abandoned like that.

"You promised," Michaela pointed her finger at him.

"I did, but are you sure you want to do this?"

"Don't worry. I'm not going to fall in love with you," she scoffed.

It was crazy, but a part of him wanted to rise to the challenge. She had his head spinning.

"I think we should take this a little slower," he said. The last thing he wanted was to have her regret tonight.

"You said you were into hot, intense and short affairs. No emotional attachment. I think this qualifies, right?"

The thought that she was thinking of this as a quick fuck bothered him. His body was all for the idea, but his conscience was bothering the hell out of him.

"You make it sound trashy." Jesus, he was acting like a chick. What was he looking for, anyway? Romance and roses?

Michaela shrugged. "It's just sex, Marcus. What's changed from five minutes ago?"

It's not just sex!

"I hadn't realized you were planning to spend your life with a man last week." Marcus wasn't sure what the hell he was doing. A night of great sex was what they both wanted.

And then there was this terrible part of him that didn't believe her. She had lied to him about where she was staying. If she was Tetsuo's spy, this would be a perfect story to keep him off center. She hadn't contacted him today. Holt said she was at Lahaina Harbor surfing, just like she told him.

"It doesn't matter," she said. "He wasn't planning to spend his life with me." Michaela balled up her napkin and stood up.

"Where are you going?" he asked.

"Don't worry. You're off the hook. I knew this was a mistake."

"Wait." He rose to his feet. "Don't go."

"Bye Marcus. Thanks for dinner." She slung her purse over her shoulder and walked out of the restaurant.

He couldn't let her leave like this, but by the time he settled the bill she was long gone. He walked up and down the beach trying to catch a glimpse of her. Marcus ran into Tetsuo instead. Just what he needed.

"Nice night, Marcus."

"If you say so."

"How is your head? I heard about your unfortunate accident."

Marcus snorted. "I bet you did. I'm fine."

"Does it hurt?"

"Not even a little bit." Marcus wondered if his smile was as psychotic as he felt right now.

"I hear they're going to open the beach in the morning."

173

"Good." He craned his neck around looking for that sexy red dress that he had been so close to taking off. What the fuck was wrong with him, anyway? So she had a fiancé, who cared? He was back where ever the hell she came from. She said he dumped her, so it wasn't like he was helping her cheat on him.

"Did you have a chance to talk to your security chief?"

"What?" Marcus brought his attention back to his arch enemy. Or what did Dude call him? Their arch enema because he was such a pain in the ass.

"About the squatters on your property."

"There are no squatters or panhandlers at Palekaiko," Marcus said.

"My sources say that you do. And you need to be aware that if you fail a housing inspection this month, I will petition to get your permits suspended. If that happens, you'll be disappointing a lot of tourists. We'll shut you down."

"Not going to happen," he said between his teeth.

Tetsuo bared his teeth in an ugly and smug smile. "I just wanted to give you fair warning. That property will be mine by summer."

"Tetsuo, I'd sell it at a loss before I sell it to you."

He shrugged. "Then I'll buy it from your buyer and make him a very rich man. Are you looking for the enchanting young woman you were eating dinner with?"

So he did know Michaela.

Marcus' fists clenched. "Where is she? If you hurt her, you will fucking regret it. I don't care who the fuck you're connected to."

"Sir?" Holt came out of the shadows and took his arm when he would have advanced on Tetsuo. It was all he could do not to shake him off. He had wanted to punch that expression off

Tetsuo's face for over two years. "You're needed back at the resort."

"Be careful who you're threatening, *haole*. Accidents happen all the time." Tetsuo tapped his own temple.

"If you go within ten feet of her..." he started to say.

"I don't care about your *yariman*."

Holt's grip tightened on him and he started to drag him away. Marcus was glad he didn't know what Tetsuo just called Michaela. But by Holt's reaction, it was pretty bad.

"If you're looking for her, she's right under your nose." Tetsuo stared at him in disdain, then nodded to Holt. "When you're ready to leave this half-ass career, you know where to find me."

"Have a nice night, Uncle."

"You can let me go now," Marcus said, after Holt had pulled him about fifty feet away.

"You can't threaten him like that. They'll cut you up alive and feed you to the sharks."

"He gets under my skin. Why was he talking about Michaela like that? What did he call her anyway?"

"Whore," Holt said blandly, not letting go of his arm or slowing their pace back to the resort.

"Cocksucker," Marcus snarled.

"There's going to be a surprise inspection tomorrow morning," Holt said.

"He's expecting to find something. So why give me warning?"

"He just wants to pull your chain. But I did some research on Michaela Harris like you wanted."

Marcus tugged his arm free and rubbed it. Holt didn't know his own strength. "What did you find out?" He felt a stab of guilt at having her investigated, but he did it with all of his lovers. He wanted to know what he was getting into.

"She's not registered under that name in any hotel in Maui."

Marcus stopped in his tracks. "She gave me an assumed name?"

Holt shrugged. "I don't think so. I think she's your squatter."

"The fuck?"

"There's been activity in the renovated rooms. I found bags in one of them. I plan on doing a raid tonight to see if I can catch the person. I've already turned off the power and water to the building."

"She hangs out with the staff. Do you think they know?"

Holt's jaw tightened. "No," he said.

Marcus nodded. "Good. We can't afford shit like that to fly. If you find out they're involved, you have my authority to fire them. Let's go to the room right now. If she's there, I'll handle it."

They walked in silence back to the hotel. Marcus was steaming from the confrontation with Tetsuo. It was still early, so people where gathered around the tiki bar. He caught his brother's attention and waved him over.

Samuel rolled his eyes and sauntered over, Amelia in tow.

"Howzit?" he said.

"Knock that shit off. Tetsuo is bringing the building inspectors and probably the housing officers over tomorrow."

Samuel looked up at Holt who nodded in confirmation.

"So?" Amelia said. "We're up to code. Let them look."

"He thinks we have a squatter. I'm going to roust her now."

"Who?" Amelia said.

"Michaela Harris."

"Why would she do that?"

"That doesn't matter now. What matters is she's stealing from us and she's about to get us in trouble."

Amelia stood in front of him. "Wait. Why are you letting Tetsuo wind you up like this? He's probably saying shit like this to get just this reaction." She waved her arms like a demented muppet.

Marcus' jaw clenched. "You're probably right. But there's no harm in checking rooms anyway."

She didn't get out of his way and side stepped with him when he went to go around her. "It's dangerous walking up there at night." Amelia pointed to the renovated rooms. "The lights are out and the workmen have tools all over the place."

"I'll put the lights back on," Holt said and left them to go to the power station.

Amelia craned her neck at him, but held out her hands to stop Marcus. "I don't want you getting hurt. Wait until he puts the lights on."

"I've got my phone as a flashlight." He brushed by her, knocking her into his brother.

"Hey," Samuel said. "Watch it, brah."

Marcus didn't bother dignifying that with an answer and clicked the flashlight app on his phone when they stepped off the lighted path. He wasn't sure why he was shaking with rage.

Questions swirled around in his mind, fueling the fire.

Had Michaela played him? Had it been all a big lie to get close to him and take his money? Or was she was squatting because she

177

didn't have anywhere to go because of asshole fiancé? She had him tied up in knots. He didn't know what to believe.

Was she a spy working for Tetsuo?

Was she a grifter?

Or was she a lonely woman on her supposed honeymoon worried about her privacy?

He almost wished it were the first two. The last one was threatening to break his heart. He gritted his teeth against the emotion.

Holt was waiting for him at the bottom of the stairs.

"Where are the lights?" he asked.

"They're really out. I just turned them off for the afternoon. When I tried to turn the power back on, nothing happens."

"Sabotage," Samuel said. "I'm getting really sick of this shit."

Amelia touched his arm. "I don't like this. It wouldn't be the first time Tetsuo has made an attempt on our lives."

"Amelia, go back to the lobby," Samuel said quietly. "Marcus, Holt, and I will handle this."

"The hell you will," she yelled at the top of her lungs. "If you're going to search this building, I'm going with you."

Marcus winced. "All right. Keep it down. You don't want to disturb the entire beach. Which room did you find the bags in?"

"305," Holt said.

"That's odd. You figure they'd squat on the ground floor," Samuel said. "Easier to get in by knocking a window or jimmying the lanai door."

"Maybe we should check the first floor first," Amelia said, her voice strident and loud in the night air.

"We'll check all the rooms. I want to see 305 first." Marcus ran up the stairs, not caring if they followed him or not. He nearly broke his ass on a saw horse and then tripped over a coil of hoses.

"Damn it."

"Are you all right?" Amelia shouted again.

"I'm fine. Calm down. And watch your step." He shone his phone at the debris. Holt strode forward with the master keys. Samuel helped Amelia through the mess. "Talk to the workers. This is unacceptable to leave this shit all over the place."

"Wait!" she screeched as Holt was about to open the door.

They all looked at her.

"What if there's a bomb in the suitcase? Shouldn't we call the police?"

"We're getting out of here right now." Samuel grabbed her arm. "Don't get blown up," he said to his brother.

"I think we should all leave," she called out in another ear deafening yell.

Samuel threw her over his shoulder and carried her down the stairs.

"It wasn't a suitcase," Holt said, "Just a bunch of shopping bags from Whaler's Inn."

He opened the door and walked in, shining his flashlight. Marcus followed. Holt went to the lanai and Marcus checked out the bathroom. Pulling open the shower curtain, he didn't see any bottles or soap. Everything seemed dry. There wasn't anything on the counter.

He came back into the main room. "Where are the bags?"

"Gone." Holt pointed his flashlight on the chair in the corner. "They were there this morning."

The bed was stripped of linens and the pillows looked untouched. Marcus opened and closed all the drawers. "Are you sure this was the right room?"

"I'm sure," he said and walked out to the lanai again. Marcus joined him.

"Well, whoever it was, they're not here now." Marcus looked out into the night. If it had been Michaela, where was she staying tonight? "See if you can find her. I'll be in my suite. Call me anytime."

Chapter Seventeen

MICHAELA HID HER HEAD IN HER HANDS. "I'm so sorry I got you guys in trouble."

"We're not in trouble yet," Joely said.

"Yeah," Makoa said. "I think we managed to get away clean."

"There wasn't much to hide," Michaela admitted.

When Joely and the boys came to her door to tell her that the jig was up, they scrambled to wipe down the shower and take every bit of evidence out of the room. She was just surprised no one broke anything climbing down from the lanai.

Loud knocking had all of them looking at each other. Joely shoved them all in the bedroom before she answered the door. All of them pressed against the bedroom door to listen.

"Where is she?" Holt said, storming inside.

"I don't know who..." Joely began.

"Stop the bullshit. I'm risking my job, here. The least you can do is be honest with me."

Joely crossed her arms and stuck out her chin at him. "You have no right to barge in here and accuse me...again."

There was a moment of charged silence. Kai whispered in Michaela's ear. "Joely holds a grudge. Holt broke up a prostitution ring a few years ago. Turned out it was her boss running it, but Joely got called in for questioning."

"Marcus gave me power to fire anyone who is aiding panhandlers and squatters."

"No one on staff is doing that."

"I can help you if you let me. Marcus wants to talk to Michaela. Do you know where she is?"

"What makes you think Michaela wants to talk to him?"

"She was having dinner with him tonight."

"Dinner's over," Joely said.

"He's worried about her," Holt said in a lower voice.

"If I see her, I'll let her know." Joely said. "Thanks for the drinks tonight."

"Yeah," he said. "Whatever."

When the door closed, they all piled out of the bedroom.

"I'd better go see what Marcus wants," Michaela said.

"You don't have to. You can stay here tonight." Joely rubbed her arms and looked at the door sadly.

"No. I stormed out on him. I'll make it right. No one is going to get fired because of me."

"Let me go make sure Holt isn't lurking around. I'll call you guys with the all clear," Hani said, and then slipped outside.

"This is all Tetsuo's fault. He still has a spy around here." Makoa smacked his fist into his palm.

"It was one thing when we knew that his nephew, Mike, was the snitch. We could feed him whatever bullshit we felt like," Kai said.

"Where's Mike now?" Michaela asked.

"He took a job on the Big Island a few months ago." Joely sat down on her couch and propped her chin up on her fist. "I wonder who Tetsuo's spy is? We haven't hired anyone new in awhile."

Michaela stared at the door. "Holt is his nephew too."

"What?" Joely gasped.

"This resort used to be owned by Holt's father. He and his brother, Mike grew up here."

"I never knew that," she said. "Did you guys know that?"

Kai shook his head.

"For the right money anyone can be bought," Makoa said.

"Not Holt," Joely scoffed.

Makoa looked at his phone. "Hani says you're good to go."

"Thanks," she said. "See you tomorrow. I hope."

Her feet still were killing her. She didn't want Marcus wondering where she'd changed, though. When she got into the elevator, she rotated her ankle while she waited to get to the top floor.

Stepping out into the hallway, she glared at the left door. She'd tell him to leave her friends alone and then leave. Then she would grab her luggage from the Kaimana Resort and catch a cab to the airport. Her boss was right. She had no business being in Maui when she had work to do back home.

Michaela squared her shoulders and knocked. The door flung open and Marcus stood there, glowering at her. He had ditched his jacket and shirt. His chest and arms were a delicious distraction.

Nope. She was going to be strong.

"I heard you were looking for me," she said with her arms crossed.

He yanked her inside and when she stumbled, he took her into his arms and kissed her. She stiffened. Who the hell did he think he was? Then, she was kissing him back. It was angry and fierce. Her nails dug into his shoulders. He had one hand on her ass and the other on the back of her head. Marcus ravaged her mouth with his tongue and teeth.

"*Okole puka*, close your damn door."

Marcus lifted his head to glare at his brother. Michaela had a dazed moment to see Samuel and Amelia in the hallway before Marcus kicked the door closed.

"Where were we?" he growled.

"That's a good question," she said, pushing out of his arms.

He let her go, but he stalked her like a jungle cat when she walked toward the window which took up the entire wall facing the ocean.

"Do you have something to say to me?" she asked.

"I want to fuck you."

His words sent a shiver down her spine. The look in his eyes was almost enough to throw herself back into his arms. "I'm mad at you," Michaela said, more to remind herself.

"I deserve it. You threw me for a loop. I was an asshole." He cupped her face in his hand. "Forgive me?"

"Not about that." She couldn't resist nuzzling his palm. It felt so good to be touched. "You're having Holt terrorize your staff trying to find me."

"Where are you staying?" Marcus said.

"It doesn't matter," she said. "I'm leaving tonight."

"Leaving the resort?"

"Leaving Maui."

"Why?" he asked.

"It was a stupid idea. I'm all alone, and I've got things to do back home."

"What kind of things?"

Michaela smirked. Might as well get it all out in the open. "I'm an attorney trying to fast track to partner."

Marcus looked like he was thinking about it. Then he shrugged. "Still want to fuck you."

She covered her hand with her mouth. She didn't want to laugh.

"One question," he said. "Are you going back because of your asshole ex?"

"Fuck no."

"Problem solved." Marcus advanced on her until she was pressed back into the window.

"Wait, what about your head?" She looked at the wound, it looked dramatically better.

"The doctor cleared me for full activities. So you're staying here tonight. All night."

"Just for tonight," she corrected. "And on one condition." She put a hand on his chest to stop him from kissing her again.

"Name it."

"No one gets fired."

"Deal. Except for that to happen, you're going to have to stay in Maui with me, here or on the boat."

She shook her head. "Tonight only."

"*Wahine*, I don't think one night is going to be enough. And I can't have you squatting in my hotel."

"There are other hotels."

He scowled at her. "I want you here where I can keep an eye on you."

She shrugged. "Maybe I'll get a room."

"We're at capacity."

"Oh well." She shrugged.

"Don't be difficult."

"One night, take it or leave it," she said.

"One night, with the option for an extension."

Was she going to do this? She'd regret it if she didn't. "Deal," she said, taking a deep breath.

"Take off that dress," he growled.

"First the shoes." Michaela kicked them off. "Ah, I've been dying to do that all night."

"Dress, now. Or I'll rip it off you."

Slipping the straps off her arms, she shimmied, and it fell into a silky pool at her feet. His sudden intake of breath made her glad she sprung for the red lace bra and matching panties.

"Your turn," she said.

He unbuttoned his pants and pushed them to his ankles, stepping out of them. His boxer briefs molded to his tight ass and did nothing to hide his hard cock.

She stepped in close and kissed him this time. His lips were as soft as his body was hard. Her heart hammered with the forbidden thrill of what she was doing. She was going to sleep with a man she'd just met a week ago for a no holds barred fling. She could be as kinky as she wanted. She could let go. She could ask for what she wanted and demand that she get it.

Swaying her hips against him, Michaela clutched his shoulders for support while their tongues tangled together. Marcus moaned in her mouth, as he slipped his hand down the back of her panties to cup her ass.

His thick erection pressed into her belly. Wiggling against it, she wanted more of it and him. Marcus was breathing heavily when he lifted his mouth from hers.

"Want you so much. You're so beautiful." He kissed down to her neck, nipping her ear.

She reached inside his underwear and gripped his cock. He sucked hard on her neck and her knees went weak.

"Marcus," she whispered.

Unhooking her bra, he captured her breasts in his hands and bent his head to lick circles over her nipples. Michaela rubbed him faster.

"Fucking going to come in your hand, if you keep doing that." He rolled her nipples between his fingers, tugging them. "You want me to come, baby?"

"Yeah," she whispered. She liked the power of having him trembling and tense so close to her.

"Get on your knees then."

Michaela sank down on the plush, white carpet, sliding his underwear down as she did. His cock was long and luscious. She licked up the shaft before taking him in her mouth.

Groaning, he pushed her head deeper and held her there. "That's it," he said.

Michaela trailed her fingernails up his thighs and stroked his balls.

"Michaela," he whispered, releasing his hold and she bobbed her head up and down on his cock. "I'm going to come down your throat, and then I'm going to eat your pussy until I'm hard again and you're screaming my name. Then, I'm going to fuck you in every position my depraved mind can think of."

She loved his dirty talk and sucked hard on him. His hips bucked and he gritted his teeth.

"Fuck, your mouth is so sweet." He held her head with both hands and pumped into her mouth. "Can't wait to feel your pussy around my cock." He gave a guttural shout of pleasure when he coated her throat. Swallowing quickly, she bobbed her head up and down him some more until his hands fell to his sides.

"Holy shit," he said and scooped her up into his arms. He carried her into the bedroom and laid her down on a big king bed. Marcus rested on his side and kissed her, while he fondled her breast.

"That was amazing," he said and moved down her body, kissing every curve and valley in her body.

Marcus licked around her belly button and along the lace edges of her panties. Spreading her legs wide, Michaela raised her hips. He pulled her underwear off and kissed her ankle. Caressing up her leg, he slowly kissed his way up it. Then kissed down the other leg to her ankle.

Michaela nearly screamed in frustration. He chuckled, the bastard.

"Something you wanted?"

"Please, lick me." Michaela wasn't above begging.

"My pleasure," Marcus said, and then he stopped fucking around. The minute his tongue entered her, she moaned and didn't stop as he tortured her clit with fast licks and then slow circles. She clutched the back of his head with both hands and fucked his face with wild thrusts. Michaela dimly thought she should be embarrassed by how she was using him to get off. But then her orgasm hit with the power of a freight train, and she couldn't do anything but feel the insane burn of pleasure as her legs jiggled out of control.

"You taste fantastic," he murmured and moved to the bedside table. He slipped on a condom and then climbed back onto the bed, kneeling between her legs.

He tickled a finger inside her. "So wet for me."

She writhed under him. Marcus's smile was full of dirty promise, and his eyes were already fucking her.

"I've been waiting for this all week."

Then he pulled her legs so she slid closer, ramming his cock to the hilt inside her. Michaela shrieked and wrapped her legs around him. Kissing her again, he took her cries of pleasure into his mouth as he pounded into her with a driving force that caused the head board to batter against the wall.

Michaela met him thrust for thrust until she was shaking again. He pinned her arms over her head as he fucked her hard and fast. Clamping down hard on his cock, her pussy spasmed as she came again. He wasn't far behind—a few more delicious long thrusts and his entire body clenched. Marcus roared as his orgasm shook over him.

She stroked all over his body. "Wow," she breathed.

Pulling out, he collapsed next to her. Tugging off the condom, he rooted around the drawer for another one. "Hold this," he said and lay on his side next to her.

"What do you want me to do with this?" she asked.

"The minute I'm hard again, put it on me and get on your hands and knees." He kissed her hard on the mouth.

Marcus stroked her clit until she was sighing, as jolts of sensations travelled down her legs. His talented mouth was busy on her nipples, tugging gently with his teeth and sucking on them. She was whimpering with need when she felt his cock hard on her hip.

"That's it," he sighed when she rolled the condom down his shaft. "Roll over."

Michaela liked his growly orders. She looked over her shoulder at him, wiggling her butt at him.

"Hang on," he warned and slammed into her from behind.

She went wild again. His hands were forceful on her hips. Marcus fucked hard, and it was just what she needed. Her breasts swayed fast and her nipples dragged on the sheet as he took her with a frenzy that she knew she'd feel well into tomorrow.

"God, yes," she said. His balls were hitting her clit with each thrust. She screamed into the pillow as the orgasm washed over her. Marcus pulled her hair at the base of her neck. She lifted her head.

"Scream again," he growled.

"Fuck, fuck, fuck!" Michaela shrieked the last word. Her body accepted everything he was giving her and begged for more. It was one continuous orgasm peaking over and over again.

Marcus grunted and fell on top of her. Kissing her shoulder, he rolled to the side and tossed the condom in the trash can with the first one.

She was boneless when he pulled her on top of him. The cool breeze from the ceiling fan dried the sweat on their bodies as he stroked her hair.

"You staying the rest of the week, *wahine*? Or do I have to do more convincing?"

"Both," Michaela murmured.

"What? No conditions this time." He yawned.

"Yeah, I got one. No business meetings. You're on vacation too."

He smirked. "I'll shove my work off on Samuel. That ought to go over well."

Michaela cuddled close to him, happier than she had been in a long time.

Chapter Eighteen

MICHAELA WOKE UP IN MARCUS' ARMS, smiling and satisfied. They made love two more times last night, and she didn't think she would be able to move today without still feeling him inside her.

"I'm going to take a shower," she said, and kissed his cheek. The stubble made him look like a sexy pirate.

Marcus made a contented noise, but didn't open his eyes. Michaela made a face at her fancy shoes as she walked by. She'd have to do the walk of shame to Joely's place to pick up her comfortable sandals and the sundress she was wearing yesterday. By check out time, she would have an official room at the Palekaiko Beach Resort, so Michaela was eager to get her things out of Tetsuo's hotel.

She stepped into Marcus' big shower and let the hot spray ease her sore muscles. As she was rinsing conditioner out of her hair, the shower door opened and a big, male body pressed up against her.

"Hi handsome," she said, turning into his arms for a good morning kiss.

"I forgot. I've got an inspection this morning from the housing department. It's all bullshit, but I need to be there. Can our vacation start this afternoon?"

Marcus soaped up her back with long, deep strokes. She reciprocated, loving the feel of his muscles.

"Yeah, that works for me. I've got to do something this morning too. How about we have a picnic on your sailboat? I was hoping to get a tour of Molokini and Lanai."

"I think that can be arranged." Marcus turned her so his erection slid between her ass cheeks.

Pouring soap down her chest, he massaged it in over her breasts. The slip slide of his hands over her nipples made her want more. Reaching around with her own sudsy hands, she stroked him.

He sucked the water off her neck, then bent her over so her palms were flat on the tile.

Easing between her thighs, he entered her inch by inch. Michaela moaned, feeling the familiar fullness. Instinctively, she gripped him. Marcus moved with slow, deliberate strokes. The shower spray rained down on her back as he gently made love to her.

Soon, she was gasping his name as pleasure danced along her spine. This orgasm was soft and drugged her with endorphins. Picking up the pace to match her demanding hips, he pulled her tightly against him.

"Yes," he gritted out, thrusting deep one final time before he came.

Straightening up, Michaela turned and wrapped her arms around his neck. "I'm glad the doctor cleared you for regular activity. When can you do strenuous?" She grinned before she kissed him.

"After lunch."

□□□

Michaela dozed in the taxi on the way to Wailea. Marcus had to skip breakfast to get to his meeting, but she grabbed a coffee and a muffin while she waited for the cab to pick her up.

The Kaimana Beach Resort was truly a diamond, but like the ring Gerald bought her, it felt cursed and the source of unhappiness. She was glad to be leaving it.

However, she did want one last view of the ocean from her balcony. Michaela opened the door to her room, and stopped dead in the doorway. Gerald was out on the balcony, having breakfast with Tetsuo.

Both of them looked up when she came in.

"What the serious fuck is going on?" she snarled, storming over.

"Michaela," Gerald rose, but thought better of leaning in for a kiss when she glared at him.

"What are you doing here?"

"It's my room," he said. "I told you I was meeting a client here."

"You're his attorney?" She pointed at Tetsuo.

"And the Kincaides as well," Tetsuo said with a smirk.

Michaela sat down hard, before she fell down. She didn't even acknowledge the scrambled eggs and bacon that was immediately put in front of her. Well, the bacon made an impression. She finished a slice before she realized she didn't want to have breakfast with these two douchebags.

"I think we can discuss business after you greeted your fiancée properly." Tetsuo rose and with a snap of his fingers, the wait staff followed.

"It's beautiful," Gerald said after they left. "I can see why you stayed."

"Cut the shit, Gerald. You have a conflict of interest representing both the Kincaides and Hojo."

He shrugged. "Officially, I'm not really Mr. Hojo's attorney."

"You're looking to get disbarred," she said.

"Grow up," he told her. "And should you really be eating another piece of bacon?"

She ate it defiantly and then took his.

"It's your ass." He leaned back in his chair.

"Were you always this much of a prick?" Michaela asked with her mouth full. "Or have I lost my immunity to it."

"I didn't come here to fight. I want to know if you thought about my offer."

She shook her head. "I already gave you my answer. It's ridiculous to force us to get married just so my father can keep it all in the family."

"I tried to talk some sense into him." Gerald waved his hand in the air in frustration. "You're welcome to try."

"Yeah, like that has ever worked. So what does Brittany think of you coming down here?"

He shrugged. "I told her it was work."

"What would you have told her if I was stupid enough to go through with this insane plan of my father's?"

"I would have told her the truth. In exchange for marrying his daughter, I get 20% of his shares in his company. You also get 20% by the way. And as far as I'm concerned, the marriage is in name only."

"She'd go for that?" Michaela frowned.

"I'd tell her we would get a divorce in five years. She'd wait for me."

"She's twenty-two. She won't wait for you."

"You have no idea about our relationship," Gerald said.

"I know she's still in love with the bass player," Michaela countered.

"How on earth would you know that?"

"We're friends on Facebook."

"That's really weird in a creepy stalker way," he said.

"Why aren't you friends with her on Facebook?" she asked.

"I don't have time for that shit."

"You should make time." Michaela pulled up Brittany's profile and handed him the phone. "I'm sure you don't care if she's still sleeping with him. After all, you have an open relationship, right?"

Marcus frowned at the phone, swiping through all of the pictures.

Leaning over, she pointed. "The one where she's doing body shots off him was my favorite."

He tossed the phone on the table. "This is stupid. It doesn't change our situation. Are you going to marry me or what?"

"No."

"Then we lose out on a lucrative stock portfolio. Your father's business is going to tank in the next five years, and my father's business won't be as successful. Everyone fails because you want to make me suffer for a moment's weakness."

Michaela's shoulders slumped. "Gerald, it's not my fault my father's being a hard ass. I might remind you that if you hadn't been bouncing Brittany on your dick and we got married as we had planned, none of this would have happened." She leaned forward again and kissed him on the cheek.

He flinched back in surprise.

"Thank you. I had been willing to settle for you. Now, I don't want to."

"Your vacation fling? Some surfer dude, I bet."

Michaela wondered why Tetsuo didn't tell Gerald she was involved with Marcus. Probably because he planned on blackmailing her with it at some point if she did agree to marry Gerald.

"Something like that." She pushed back from the table. "I'm going to get changed and pack my clothes. Then I'm out of here."

"Are you going back home?" he asked.

"Something like that," she said again. It was none of his damn business.

"Try to talk some sense into your father, please?"

"No way."

"Then think about getting married. The only thing that would change is everybody would get rich."

Michaela closed the door to the balcony, shutting him out of her life once and for all.

Chapter Nineteen

THE INSPECTION WAS BULLSHIT AND THEY found nothing out of the ordinary. Marcus expected nothing less, but he still high-fived his brother after they left.

"I'm going to be out on the boat for a while. Maybe a couple of days. Can I borrow Gregson?" Marcus said, hoping Samuel wasn't going to bust his balls.

"You and the teeny bikini going to go to Molokini?"

Marcus rolled his eyes. "How long have you been waiting to say that?"

"All week, brah. All week. Sure. Just have him stock the fridge on the *Hedge Fun* before he goes. Amelia loves his shrimp salad."

"Thanks." Marcus called Gregson, but happened to look up to see Holt bearing down on them like a steam roller.

"You deal with that," Samuel said. "I'm going to do snorkel lessons or something."

Marcus hung up and slid his phone into his pocket.

"I need to see you in private. Can you come to my office?"

"Sure." Marcus followed Holt, unease filling him. "Is everything all right?"

"Nope. Not even one little bit." Holt sat behind his desk and motioned Marcus to look over his shoulder.

"Tetsuo sent us these pictures today."

"Why the fuck would I…" Marcus cut off mid-sentence when he recognized Michaela's hair flying in the wind. She was seated on a balcony with his lawyer, Gerald Stone, and Tetsuo.

Gerald Stone.

Gerald.

A week ago today Gerald left me at the altar.

Had that been true? If so, what was she doing with him now?

In the picture, she was leaning over him and smiling at something that was on his phone. In another she kissed his cheek. It certainly didn't look like there were any hard feelings. Marcus tried to control his breathing and his temper.

"Do you recognize where they are?" Holt asked.

He shook his head.

"It's the Kaimana Beach Resort. The reason I couldn't find a Michaela Harris was because the room is under Michaela and Gerald Stone."

Marcus leaned a hip against Holt's desk, tearing his eyes from the photo of her kissing his attorney. "So she's married?"

The next picture Holt brought up was the couple with Tetsuo.

"What's my lawyer doing with meeting with Tetsuo? Staying in his hotel?" Laughing with my girl?

"Tetsuo said that they are in the bridal suite and he was paying respects to the bride and groom. But I think that's bullshit."

Marcus whipped his gaze to him. "Why?"

"Because my uncle doesn't do anything without a reason. He knows who Gerald Stone and Michaela Harris-Stone are to you. He's playing mind games."

"It's working," Marcus said.

"Then stop playing. I don't know what's going on with the Stones. You need to fire your lawyer and ditch the girl."

"They're both lawyers," Marcus said suddenly.

"What?"

"She told me last night. Do a google search for Michaela Harris, attorney in California. Let's see if she lied about that."

Marcus knew he was grasping at straws, but he needed to know if at least one thing she said to him was the truth. Her name popped up along with her firm and a few cases that she worked on.

"Well, at least she's not a transient," Holt said, laconically. "Or after your money."

"She's working for Tetsuo, isn't she?"

When Holt didn't say anything, Marcus turned and punched the wall. "That's why we can't get anywhere. He's my lawyer and she's his. Son of a bitch."

Rage filled him, burning away the hurt and confusion. "I want all the department heads in the board room in a half hour. Include the bell staff too. We're going to shut that bitch down now." He slammed out of the room.

□□□

Marcus was back to chewing Tylenol again, but this time the pain had nothing to do with his throbbing head. It was torture to listen to everyone defend Michaela to him. Even after they saw the pictures.

"We tried to plant false information with her and as far as we could tell, she never gave it to Tetsuo," Samuel said.

"That's because she knew it was bullshit." Marcus was on his fifth cup of coffee and even though it was ripping his insides up, it was keeping his temper on a fine edge.

"She went to the law library to find dirt on him." Amelia turned her laptop towards him. "I've got all her notes."

"That was to throw us off the trail," Marcus said. "She's smart and vicious, like a shark."

"I called her office," Holt said. "I talked to her paralegal. I pretended I was a new client and I said I wanted to know when she was back from her honeymoon."

Marcus grit his teeth.

"The paralegal said, she'd be back next Monday."

"She said he jilted her at the altar," Hani said. "She was in tears at the front desk. He canceled the reservations."

"Why wasn't I aware my attorney had booked a room here?" Marcus asked with deadly sweetness.

"I don't know who your attorney is," Hani said.

"She's a very good actress," Marcus said, staring down the anger in Hani's eyes. "I don't blame you for being duped. But we found our spy. She's not allowed on the premises. Call me when she shows up and I will escort her out of here personally."

"I can do that," Amelia said.

"No. You cannot." Marcus told her.

Samuel put his hand on his wife's shoulder.

"None of this makes sense." Joely was in tears. "She was our friend."

"No, she wasn't," Marcus said.

Joely looked miserable. She glanced over at Amelia, pleadingly.

Amelia nodded. "I have a confession to make."

Marcus rolled his eyes. "I know this is Sunday, but we're not in church. You want to tell me about a mistake you made?"

Amelia's eyes flashed fire, but he didn't care. He was in the mood for a fight and if he riled her up enough, Samuel would have a go at him.

"When Michaela arrived, I put her in room 305 until we had a room available. She was our squatter. No one else knew, but me. The fault is all mine. So if you want to fire me, go ahead."

Marcus' jaw was starting to hurt from clenching his teeth so hard.

"Oh babe," Samuel said. "Why didn't you tell me?"

"Since when do you care about the guests?" She shook off his arm. "I believe her. That woman was devastated. Her asshole of a fiancé dumped her and then cancelled the reservation."

"That's because he had rooms booked at the Kaimana Resort."

"Then why did she show up here?"

"Tetsuo sent her to spy on us. Maybe even sabotage the renovations."

"He would have no idea that we could find her a room. Or that I would put her in an illegal room."

"Amelia, he knows you. Your previous situation would have colored your judgement. They played you. You were taken for a fool. Admit it and move on."

"Go to hell," she snarled and grabbed her laptop as she sped out of the room.

"Thanks a lot, dickhead." Samuel followed her out.

"If there isn't any more questions, you all have your instructions." He also stood up and moved to the door. "Let's all do better next time."

Marcus refrained from slamming it on his way out.

Chapter Twenty

MICHAELA WAS GETTING A LITTLE BORED with the scenery from Wailea to Kaanapali. Marcus wasn't answering his phone. She hoped everything had gone all right with the inspection.

When she got out of the cab and wheeled her bag into the lobby, she felt as if her vacation had finally started. Hani didn't look up as she approached and after a moment she said, "Checking in."

"I'm sorry," he said without meeting her eyes. "There isn't a reservation in your name."

"Seriously? No one has checked out yet?" Michaela sighed. "Oh well, can you stow these in the back and I'll go see if I can find Marcus."

"If you have a seat, I'll call him for you."

"Thanks. He doesn't seem to be answering his phone."

Hani must be really busy, she thought and sat down in one of the lobby chairs. It wasn't as posh as the Kaimana, but it felt like home.

"He'll be right with you," Hani said and went back to brooding at his screen.

She didn't have long to wait. Marcus strode into the lobby. The welcoming smile on her face died when she saw his expression.

"Call Mrs. Stone a cab," he said, hauling her up by her upper arm to her feet.

"On its way," Hani said sullenly.

"What are you doing?" she asked as Marcus picked up her luggage and carried it to the taxi stand outside. "And why did you call me Stone? That's Gerald's last name."

"Oh, so you admit that Gerald Stone is your husband?"

"No," she said. "He's the jack ass that left me at the altar last week."

"Then why were you having breakfast with him this morning in Tetsuo Hojo's bridal suite. A suite that's registered to Mr. and Mrs. Stone."

"Oh for fuck's sake," Michaela groaned. "That's the son of a bitch's angle."

"Yeah, you know all about angles don't you Attorney Stone."

"Attorney Harris. If you're going to be a jerk, at least call me by my legal name."

"So you didn't take his name when you got married?"

"I'm not married. He got cold feet." She peered up at him. "Did you hit your head again?"

"I'm fine. I'm sick of you dodging my questions, though. Why were you eating breakfast with him?"

"I wasn't."

"I have pictures of it," he seethed.

"I'm sure you do. But what you saw was me collecting my luggage and coming back here to check in."

"To get closer to me?"

"Shit yeah, I was looking to get a lot closer to you, but now I'm wondering if that was a mistake."

"It was," he sneered. "The worst mistake of your life."

"No," Michaela shook her head. "That's still Gerald. Can we go somewhere private and have a cup of coffee?"

Makoa, Hani and Kai ducked back into their hiding spots when Marcus started to pace. She managed not to roll her eyes at them.

"Why so you can seduce me again?"

"That's the last thing on my mind." She poked him in the chest. "And you did all the seducing, Buster. Every single time. You started it." She paused. "Except for that time in Ho'okipa, but I owed you for that one."

Hani looked up and raised his eyebrow at her.

Clenching his fists in frustration, Marcus turned away. "Where were you staying for the past week?"

She caught Hani's eye and he nodded. No. She wasn't going to get them in trouble. Not when Marcus was being this irrational.

"I was in Wailea."

"You're a liar." Marcus turned back and loomed over her. For a minute, she was frightened by the look in his eyes. "I can't trust you. I don't even know if I want to. You're no longer welcome here. If you're caught on the property again, I'll have you arrested for trespassing. And tell your husband, he's fired."

Michaela's mouth dropped open in shock. He was walking away from her. He kicked her out of the resort. Makoa put her bags in the taxi cab and hugged her quickly.

Amelia hurried out of the lobby, looking over her shoulder. She pressed her ring box into her hand. "He'll calm down once he starts thinking with his big head instead of his little one."

"I'm not a spy," Michaela said.

"I know. We all know. Except for him."

"Amelia!" Marcus thundered.

Amelia rolled her eyes. "Seriously? Does he think I'm going to respond to that tone? Even if he could fire me, I'd tell him to go shit in his hat. You take care." She hugged her.

"I'm sorry, if I got you in trouble." Michaela sniffed as tears threatened. "You were so kind to me. I'll never forget that."

"I hate him. He's a dick," Amelia wailed.

The taxi beeped his horn.

"Bye. Tell everyone, thank you."

Kai and Hani had already scattered. She didn't even get to say good-bye to them or to Joely.

□□□

Gerald was still on the balcony when she got back. She sat down across from him. Michaela felt cold inside, even though the day was as sunny and perfect as she could imagine.

"All right," she said.

"I knew you'd come to your senses. We make a great team. I was thinking, maybe this marriage could be real after all." He reached out for her hand but she snatched it away.

"No." Anger burned away the last of the numbness. She cried her heart out in the taxi cab, there was no more of that emotion left. "Here's how it's going to be. We'll take the 20% stock options. We both sign a pre-nup. In the case of a divorce, we split everything 50/50, keeping what we came into the marriage with. We'll divorce once my father passes away or five years, whichever is sooner. Do we have a deal?"

Gerald blinked. "Yes. Absolutely. I'll have the papers drawn up."

"There will be no sex. No intimacy. No nothing. We'll live in separate residences. You keep your condo and your girlfriend and I'll keep my condo." And my nothing else. Michaela furiously pushed that thought aside. She wouldn't remember the mind shattering sex, the tender love making, or surfing on the blue Maui shore with Marcus.

Gerald nodded. "Agreed. If that's what you want."

"As far as I'm concerned this will be a purely business relationship. I will keep my own name. You can spend holidays with whomever you want. I don't care."

"This doesn't have to be a hostile merger," he said, trying to make a joke.

"But by its very nature it is. I am being strong armed into a loveless marriage for profit. I'm sick of fighting. I'll do it, but it's going to be on my terms."

"I'm still your friend," he said.

"You never were my friend." Michaela looked out into the sea. She had thought there were no more tears. Her friends were back at the Palekaiko Beach Resort. Joely, Amelia, Kai, Hani, and Makoa. And she would never see them again.

Wiping the tears from her eyes, she realized she had one more condition. "I want you to dump Tetsuo Hojo as a client." Marcus could fire Gerald on his own time. She wasn't his employee to be ordered around.

"He pays me a lot of money," Gerald hedged.

"It's a deal breaker for me. How bad do you want the merger?"

Gerald stared her down for a full minute. Whatever he saw in her eyes, he didn't try and negotiate or bargain. "Fair enough. I think he'd rather have you on retainer than me anyway. You're all he could talk about this week. Are you going to take the bar here?"

"No," she said. "There's nothing for me in Maui." She deliberately turned her back on the waves.

"Well, I for one, am glad to have the old Michaela back. This will all blow over and things will get back to normal as soon as our vacation is done." He went to kiss her on the temple, but she flinched away from him.

"I'm leaving on a four o'clock flight. You can drive me to the airport."

"Honey, we have this room for a whole week."

"I'm going home," she said. "Fly your girlfriend out."

He shrugged. "If you insist. I'm going to go take a shower."

When he was gone, Michaela unclenched her fist and opened the abused ring box. The pretty, sparkly diamond winked up at her. She slid the cursed thing on her finger. They were stuck with each other now.

As she was getting up from the table, Gerald's email beeped. Looking over her shoulder, Michaela confirmed he was in the shower. She sat in his chair. It was an email from Marcus. She deleted it unread. Marcus didn't get to be a shit heel in email. She wanted him to scream at Gerald over the phone or in person like he did to her.

It wasn't fair that Tetsuo was going to keep putting the screws to her friends, though. No matter how she and Marcus ended, they didn't deserve to be collateral damage. She logged onto her email and sent Amelia a message to open up the documents she was about to send to her from Gerald's email account.

Then Michaela found every single piece of correspondence she could find pertaining to Tetsuo Hojo and emailed it to Amelia. It was a huge ethics violation. But technically, Gerald was still the Kincaides' lawyer. Amelia was a Kincaide. She knew that Gerald had been charged with finding everything he could on how to stop Tetsuo in his tracks. Michaela liked to think she was forcing Gerald to do his due diligence.

Then she deleted the emails from his sent folder. She heard the shower go off, and she knew she didn't have much more time. She hoped she had given the Kincaides' next lawyer some ammunition.

Chapter Twenty-One

MICHAELA REFUSED TO EVEN GET the dress on until Gerald's sister, Corrine, sent her a picture of Gerald at the church, in his tuxedo. Only then, did she allow her other bridesmaids to help her get dressed and into the limousine.

Her father had been able to book the same church and the same reception hall almost a month and a half to the day of the last fiasco. Of course, Michaela had wanted to have the justice of the peace perform the civil ceremony and be done with it, but her father wouldn't hear of it.

Michaela was done arguing. He bought the dress. She'd wear the dress. He'd booked the venues. She'd show up. As long as Gerald did.

She had a terrible feeling of déjà vu when she stood in the vestibule and peeked out, but there was Gerald. He was laughing with his best man by the altar. Her terrible feeling just grew worse. She had invited her friends from the Palekaiko Resort, hoping that they would come. But they hadn't. It had been a long shot. Air fare was expensive and the resort probably couldn't afford to have all of them take time off at the same time, even if she did dangle a trip to Mavericks to sweeten the pot. It wasn't as if Gerald and she were going on a honeymoon. After the reception, they were going back to their respective condos.

Squinting at the groom's side of the church, she caught sight of Brittany. That was some balls, there. I guess that's what Gerald was doing when this horrible day was over. She had a few pints of Ben and Jerry's in the fridge waiting for her. It wasn't malasadas, but it would do the trick.

Michaela had hoped Amelia would have dragged Samuel to the wedding. Well, if she was being honest, she had hoped that Amelia would have told Marcus about the wedding. But if she did, he didn't call or attempt to contact her. She had wanted a chance to explain everything and just talk, but apparently that ship had sailed.

She hoped the information she sent to them helped. Michaela didn't like Tetsuo's machinations and was glad to throw a wrench into them.

"I'm sorry. This is a private party," she heard her father tell someone who walked in. By the tone of his voice, it wasn't anyone who had been invited.

"I'm here to give the bride a gift." Michaela's fingers went white knuckled on the door. Surely, she didn't hear that voice correctly. Turning around, she thought Dude had come to the wedding after all. But it was Marcus, dressed in board shorts and a Hawaiian shirt. He wore sunglasses and a beer bottle dangled from one hand. Under his arm was a large, rectangle package.

"You can put that with the rest of the presents, and they'll be transported to the reception."

"Can you give us a few moments, Dad?" she asked.

"The wedding is going to start in fifteen minutes." He pulled back his sleeve and checked his watch.

"That's all I'll need," Marcus said.

Her father audibly sniffed as he passed Marcus, never suspecting that one of People Magazine's most eligible billionaires was standing two feet away.

"You look beautiful," Marcus said.

"I know." Michaela took the beer bottle out of his hand and drained the rest of it. "My stylist took four hours on my hair and

211

make-up." She belched behind her hand. "I'm a freaking goddess. What do you want, Kincaide?"

"Open it," he said.

"Is it ticking?" She shook the box, experimentally.

He flashed a sexy grin that Michaela told herself she was immune to. It was wrapped with a wide, white silk bow. If she thought she could get away with it, she would stuff it in her purse. That way, if she needed courage today, she could reach in and stroke it and remember that a part of Maui was with her.

Carefully, she set it aside and placed her purse down on top of it. Michaela was pretty sure she could scoop the ribbon in without him seeing her do it. She opened the box and pushed away the tissue paper. It was a wet suit.

Pulling it out, she noticed it had a pocket for a CO_2 bottle. It was an inflatable wet suit, so if you got hammered by the waves you had a chance of getting help floating back to the surface. "I've wanted one of these forever," she said. "They've always been backordered."

"Why don't you try it on and we can hit Hermosa Beach? I hear the waves are choice today."

She blinked at him. "I'm getting married today."

"Wouldn't you rather go surfing?"

Yes. Yes, she would. But that was beside the point. "I don't think you can handle the waves here, Hawaii boy. That water is fucking cold."

"That's what the wet suit is for."

"Do you have another beer?"

"I've got everything you want on my boat. It's docked in Marina del Rey."

She swallowed hard and looked away. "I get it. You think this would be a great way to get revenge on Gerald and Tetsuo. I'll save you the trouble. They couldn't care less."

Marcus nodded, grabbed her by the arm and pulled her into the coat closet, shutting the door behind him. Unfortunately, half her train was on the other side of the door.

"What on earth?" Michaela had just enough time to say that before his mouth was on her and he was kissing her with that same Maui magic that made her fall in love with him.

She knew she was in love with the stupid jerk when she couldn't stop thinking about him over the past month. It was a bad idea to continue this kiss, but it felt too good to stop. The scruff on his cheeks were silky soft and she quivered against him as she remembered how it felt between her legs.

Marcus fumbled at the buttons on the back of her dress. "How many of these damned things are there?"

"Over a hundred," she said and brought his head down to hers again.

He gave up on the buttons as their tongues tangled. He tried to lift her skirts to get his hand under them, but there were too many layers.

"Fuck," he said in annoyance, breaking off the kiss. He turned her around and went back to the buttons.

By the time Michaela's head stopped spinning, he was making headway. "Stop," she said. "Do you know how long it took them to get me into this contraption?"

"You can't surf in this. But more importantly," he leaned in and nipped her earlobe. "You can't fuck in it."

He had enough of the buttons done so he could pull her arms out of the sleeves and push the dress down to her waist. Ravaging her neck, he caressed her breasts over the corset she wore.

"You can leave this on," he groaned and went back to unbuttoning.

"You can't fuck me silly in fifteen minutes and then have me walk down the aisle."

"It's more like ten minutes now. And you're not getting married today."

"I'm not?" she asked in a small voice.

He turned her around again and got the dress buttons open so he could push the dress around her waist. "Tell me you want to marry Gerald and I'll button you back up and leave."

Michaela clutched his arms. "Don't you fucking dare."

He turned her back around to continue the buttons. "I'm sorry. I'm a hot headed idiot. I should have calmed down and gone out to coffee with you. I should have realized Tetsuo was playing games."

"He was playing games with all of us," she said softly.

"My problem is I fell for you fast and hard and all I could think was that it was one-sided."

Michaela shook her head. "No, it wasn't."

"I've been a raging asshole these past few weeks. And it's because I knew I fucked up and I didn't think I could fix it with a phone call. This was the only way I thought I could." He turned her back around. She was beginning to get dizzy. This time, he was able to push the dress to her ankles.

Marcus helped her step out of it.

"Holy shit," he muttered.

She was wearing white stockings and a matching garter belt. The corset pushed her breasts up and rested just below her panties. Of course, the ensemble was ruined by the fact she was wearing white Chuck Taylors instead of heels.

"I love you," he said. "We only had a week together and some of that was crazy times. But I've never felt this way about anyone before. I don't know if this will last or if the feelings will get stronger. All I know is I can't let you marry Gerald Stone and I can't let another minute go by when I'm not inside you."

Michaela launched herself at him, wrapping her legs around him. Marcus staggered, nearly tripped over her gown, but found his balance and pressed her against the wall. He pulled a condom out of his pocket as he kissed her into a frenzy. Pulling his board shorts down, he put it on. Marcus tickled his finger against her clit and she moaned.

"You're so wet and ready for me," he whispered.

"Always," she whispered back.

He plunged inside her, taking her hard and fast against the closet wall. Never once did he stop kissing her. The wall creaked and shook. His cock stretched her, filled her with every satisfying stroke. She bucked and writhed, wanting more needing everything he could give her. When she came screaming, it was only his mouth on hers that stopped anyone from coming to investigate. He was right behind her, coming with a satisfied grunt.

"Holy shit," he said again, resting his forehead against hers.

"I love you," she whispered against his mouth. "I know it's too soon and too crazy, but you're right. We need to give this a chance."

"Come away with me. Sail on my yacht until you're sick of me. I want to wake up next to you and make love all day long."

"What about your hotels?" she asked.

"Samuel can fill in when we don't have wireless. Take a leave of absence from work. Or quit outright. Unless," he looked up at her. "You really want to be partner. Then we'll figure out another way. I can run my business from California as easy or easier than I could from Maui. We got cheated. I want two weeks with you. Two months, if you let me. Two years, if we want. Whatever it takes, until its forever. What do you say?"

"Let's go grab some waves."

Her parents gaped at them as they came out of the church hand in hand.

"What is going on here?" her father thundered.

"I'm Marcus Kincaide," he said. "I love your daughter."

"Marcus Kincaide, the hotelier?" her mother asked.

"Yes, Ma'am. There's not going to be a wedding today."

"Now, see here..." her father started to say, but Michaela interrupted him.

"No, you listen. Gerald Stone is a bad match for me. He's one step from being disbarred because of his questionable ethic practices. You wouldn't want that staining the reputation of your company, would you?"

Her father frowned, "Of course not, but..."

Michaela cut him off again. "Marcus is a successful businessman. He's honest and hardworking and I love him too."

"When did this happen?" her mother wailed.

"It happened fast. Almost too fast to be real. So we're going to take a few months off to make sure," Michaela said.

"But the church, the reception..." Her father looked lost.

Michaela twisted off her engagement ring. "This is worth ten grand. I don't want it. But listen to me. Not as a daughter, but as an attorney. Merging with Stone Mechanics is the right thing to do financially for the future of your company. Do it. Just leave me out of it, okay?"

"But it's my legacy. I want my grandchildren to have it one day."

"Then leave them your shares in it. I've got to go." She stood up on tiptoes and kissed his cheek. "Take care of him," she said to her mom and kissed her too.

"Michaela, you have a church full of guests," her father thundered.

"Darling, please don't shout. I have a headache. Can you fix me a nice martini? There's a good boy." Her mother patted his arm. "Be happy dear." She waved at them.

And for the second time, Michaela ran out of the church in her underwear. Except this time, she had a wetsuit in one hand and a handsome surfer dude in the other.

Epilogue

One year later

"WELL, THEY SAY THIRD TIME'S THE CHARM," her father grumbled. They stood on the beach, both of them barefoot. He wore the loudest Hawaiian shirt she had ever seen and khaki shorts that showed off his knobby knees.

Michaela wore a haku lei of white flowers on her head instead of a veil and her white sundress was light and airy. Her mother and Zarafina toasted them with Mai Tais as they walked down the beach in a makeshift aisle. Paper bags filled with battery powered tea lights ran the length of it. The aisle ended at the stone palm trees where Dude hung his hammock, Marcus stood with his best man, Holt. They were dressed in more sedate Hawaiian shirts and slacks. Marcus was so handsome. Her surfer business man. Together they found the compromise that made them both happy. Her face hurt from grinning.

Her maid of honor, Joely was also at the front in a green halter dress. Dude was officiating, having taken the necessary online course to be declared a minister. He wore a simple black shirt with a gold palm tree on the back and matching pants. Of course, he was also barefoot. He had a wicked gleam in his eyes that she didn't quite trust.

Amelia was still running around, making sure everything was perfect. Michaela wasn't sure what she was worried about. Tetsuo had his hands full with all the paperwork she had been filing in the local courts. He wouldn't be bothering them for a long time, if ever.

Michaela could smell the roasted pig as the catering staff of the Palekaiko Beach Resort set the tables in the tiki bar. Her wedding cake was a sticky confection of malasadas held together with honey and spun sugar. She wanted to skip to the cake cutting ceremony.

"This is the wedding I've always dreamed of," she said.

"It better be," her father grumbled. "This is the last time I'm walking you down the aisle."

"We've got a life here now," she said. "I've opened up my own law firm and Marcus is running all of his projects from here. I think you can safely assume your father of the bride responsibilities are over."

Her father handed her off to Marcus and went to stand next to her mother.

"Yo! Listen up," Dude started.

"You're not going to do it like this. You promised." Marcus glanced over at their mother but she just shrugged and kept taking pictures.

"I'm so sorry," Marcus muttered to Michaela.

"We knew what we were getting into," Michaela said.

"Today we gonna join dis bruddah and the wahine with the teeny bikini..."

"I'm going to going to shove your snorkel fins so far up your ass, you're going to have the stick out your tongue to paddle," Marcus said between his teeth.

"Catherine, what's going on?" her father asked.

"Hush, Harold. This is the way they do things on the island." She flipped the shaka at Samuel. "Preach it, Dude."

"Is it early to start drinking?" Michaela asked Marcus out of the corner of her mouth.

Samuel raised his hands over the two of them. "Do you hupo take this lolo to be your bride?"

"Did he just call me stupid?" Michaela asked.

"You are marrying him," Samuel pointed out.

"Yes," Marcus snapped.

"Sistah, are you sure about dis?"

"Yes."

"Well, then kiss her and I don't wanna see any tongue."

"Close your eyes then," Marcus said, pulling Michaela to him.

As usual, she melted into his arms and everything faded away. She was home. It was perfect.

"Since you pledged your eternal alohas to each other, by da mana I possess, I pronounce you Pilikua and Pilialo." Dude finished with a flourish. "Now let's go eat. Dey gonna be a while."

"Aloha au 'ia 'oe," Michaela whispered to Marcus.

"I love you too." Marcus kissed his bride again.

The End

To learn more about the great island of Maui and what it offers, check out these links:

Pride of Maui

http://www.prideofmaui.com/blog/maui/best-malasadas-maui.html

Maui Guidebook

http://mauiguidebook.com/beaches/hookipa-beach-park/

How to talk like a surfer

http://www.surfing-waves.com/surf_talk.htm

Useful Hawaiian words

http://www.howtoliveinhawaii.com/1023/35-hawaiian-words-every-new-resident-should-know/

For a sneak peek at how **Beach My Life**'s hero, Holt Kawena, grew up, read all about the Hawaiian cowboys, the *paniolos*, here:

http://www.nytimes.com/2013/10/06/travel/in-mauis-upcountry-where-the-paniolo-roam.html?_r=0

If you want to find out how to make malasadas, Saveur Magazine, has a feature from a famous Hawaiian malasada maker, Leonard's Bakery. Read the article here:

http://www.saveur.com/article/Recipes/Hawaii-Malasadas

FREE BOOK

Thank you! I hope you enjoyed this book and would consider leaving me a review.

If you'd like to keep up-to-date on my new releases and other fun things, please subscribe to my newsletter and get a *FREE BOOK*.

Be a VIP Reader and have a chance to win monthly prizes, free books and up-to-date information.

Your Free Book:

Click Here:

https://dl.bookfunnel.com/w9gnkxp12u

More Books by Jamie K. Schmidt

If you liked this book, you may want to try:

Three Sisters Ranch Series
(high heat contemporary romance)

USA Today Best Seller: The Cowboy's Daughter

The Cowboy's Hunt

The Cowboy's Heart

A Cowboy for April

A Cowboy for June

A Cowboy for Merry – coming soon

Club Inferno Series
(erotic contemporary romance)

USA Today Best Seller: Heat

Longing

Fever

Passion – coming 2022

The Emerging Queens Series
(high heat paranormal romance)

The Queen's Mystery – FREE when you sign up to be a VIP reader

The Queen's Wings

The Queen's Plight

The Queen's Flight

The Queen's Dance

The Queen's Gambit – coming soon

The Queen's Conclave – coming soon

The Truth & Lies Series
(erotic New Adult romance)

Truth Kills

Truth Reveals

The Hawaii Heat series
(high heat contemporary romance)

USA Today Best Seller: Life's a Beach

Beach Happens

Beach My Life

Beauty and the Beach

The Sentinels of Babylon series
(high heat contemporary romance)

Necessary Evil

Sentinel's Kiss

Warden's Woman

Ryder's Reckoning

Stand-alone novels
(high heat contemporary romance)

2018 Rita® Finalist in Erotic Romance: Stud – Retitled *Extra Whip*

Hard Cover

Maiden Voyage

Spice - Book Three in the Fate Series - Co-written with Jenna Jameson

Wild Wedding Hookup

Holiday Hookup

Stand-alone novels & novellas

Trinity (erotic ménage paranormal romance)

Midnight Lady, (high heat fantasy romance)

Naked Truth (romantic suspense)

Santa Genie (erotic paranormal romance)

Samurai's Heart (erotic paranormal romance)

Betrayed (erotic fantasy romance)

The Handy Men (erotic ménage romance)

Shifter's Price (erotic ménage dystopian paranormal romance)

The Seeker (paranormal romance)

A Spark of Romance (sweet small town romance)

Newsletter Subscriber's First Peek

A Casual Christmas (contemporary romance) – Exclusive to newsletter subscribers for 2017. Now available.

A Not So Casual Christmas (contemporary romance) – Exclusive to newsletter subscribers for 2018. Now available.

A Chaotic Christmas (contemporary romance) – Exclusive to newsletter subscribers for 2019. Now available.

A Second Chance Christmas (contemporary romance) – Exclusive to newsletter subscribers for 2020. Now available.

The Gingerbread Cowboy – Exclusive to newsletter subscribers for 2021. Available wide in October 2022.

Sign up_ here www.jkschmidt.com/newsletter to receive the 2022 short story The Candy Cane Cowboy FREE on Christmas Eve. It will be exclusive to newsletter subscribers until October 2023.

Anthologies & Collections

Graveyard Shift (High heat paranormal romance)

Flash Magic (No heat at all speculative fiction stories)

Made in the USA
Las Vegas, NV
03 August 2024

93292127R00128